Four
Ways of
Computing
Midnight

Four
Ways of
Computing
Midnight

FRANCIS PHELAN

Atheneum   NEW YORK   *1985*

SCRIBNER
Rockefeller Center
1230 Avenue of the Americas
New York, NY 10020

Portions of this book previously appeared in *The Southern Review*,
The Georgia Review, and the *University of Windsor Review*.

Lines from "Children of Light" by Robert Lowell in *Lord Weary's
Castle*, copyright 1946, 1974 by Robert Lowell. Reprinted by permission
of Harcourt Brace Jovanovich, Inc.; Lyrics from "This Was a Real Nice
Clambake" by Richard Rodgers and Oscar Hammerstein II, copyright
1945 by Williamson Music, Inc. Copyright renewed. Sole selling agent—
T. B. Harms Company (% The Welk Music Group, Santa Monica, CA
90401). International copyright secured. All rights reserved. Used by
permission.

Manufactured in the United States of America
10 9 8 7 6 5 4 3 2 1

Library of Congress Cataloging-In-Publication Data

Phelan, Francis.
        Four ways of computing midnight.

        I. Title.
PS366H35F6   1985   813'.54   84-18610
ISBN: 0-7432-4537-7

For information regarding the special discounts for bulk purchases, please contact Simon &
Schuster Special Sales at 1-800-456-6798 or business@simonandschuster.com

To all prisoners of the barbed wire

Contents

Four
Ways of
Computing
Midnight

☒ INTROIT

October 2, 1984

Dear Anne Francis,

I am responding to the article printed in the Examiner *about you and your husband. I am 55 years old and my father left a Religious order, at first just to get away, I guess. Then he met my mother—they were both 40 years old, and they would soon have three little girls and a boy. I was the youngest. Not one of the little children knew about his secret.*

Then when I was eight years old I went to a girl's camp for two weeks. The camp owned a yacht and the young man who took care of it told me about my dad, whom I loved more than life itself. Well, if you had driven a hot poker through my little heart it could not have hurt more. I didn't tell anyone, ever. I was 35 when he died.

Some of his relatives came to the funeral from a neighboring state. Because I cared for my dad at home, (I was the nurse in the family) my Uncle gave me an envelope and said, "Don't open it now, but sometime when you're alone." And sure as I am living and breathing there was a photograph of my father, all in black and with a white Roman collar. This confirmed what that young man had told me so many years before.

As I was reading that little piece in the paper about you and your husband, I asked myself the question—you were in a way trapped in a very high position. But being a Nun is not a sacrament, so with a lot of convincing you can get out. Is that it?

But I am trapped in a 34 year old marriage. I've been down every avenue and, short of suicide, there is no way out. My friend who was a Nun tells me I don't have enough faith, and it's true. I'm not the good little Catholic I was in training. I remember going into our little chapel and it was like being transported. I would feel as light as air.

Now I am in a living hell and no one but God can help me; He must have a very good reason not to.

I've read so many times that we are born free and that we make our own mistakes.

Pray for me when you can.

℥ *DISPUTATIO*

"Tell again what God it was that set the conflict. Who brought on this bitter battle?"
—*Iliad*, line 10

"Well, I will start afresh and once again make dark things clear."
—*Oedipus Tyrannus*, line 132

Dear Next, My Dear Same,

Your letter on its green, lined writing paper was sent to my wife, Anne Francis. But you left it unsigned, and since it had no return address, we could not answer, no matter how much we wanted to.

But I had a dream, and in my dream the green lines of the paper had become wires and coils, and the handwriting had become like a little bird, fluttering against the wires—and, I could see, caught on them. In the dream Anne Francis and I were with a group of people, escaping. When we were free I turned and looked back, and saw something hanging from the barbed wire, like empty clothes, waving in the wind. Then, Anonymous, I saw that it was you, and you were hanging from the barbed wire. "Oh my Next!" I shouted. "My poor Next!"

5

Anne Francis will answer in her own way, perhaps. These are my answers; the dream made me want to write them down for you, even though you may never read them, will never know why I call you "Next."

But something keeps happening, Anonymous. Because you do not tell me who you are as you ask "Why?" and "How?" you have a way of turning into all sorts of things on me. Because you do not own up to who you are, you become people you would never recognize. You start off simply enough, as the casual Enquirer, or even the Examiner, but quickly enough, soon enough, you turn into the Questioner, the Interrogator, and, yes, before it is over, the Inquisitor, even the grand old Inquisitor himself. Yet there is something about you: I know you are not going to do anything about your own case, which is not—Semblable—so different from mine.

The one I am least offended with is Hamlet. Oh, I know you never meant to be Hamlet, Next—but I see such good reasons for it. You see, Hamlet is a young member of a House of Theology, a House of Philosophy, where they do the Disputation. He is home on leave, but still practices his Disputatio. *He wants to know what the Question is, what is the week's Question nailed up on the board for debate. In the* Disputatio *it is always stated in the Latin form—Utrum/An?, Whether/Or? First he "puts" the Question: it is "To Be/Or Not?" Then he appoints himself Defensor Thesis. He lists the Objections in proper order, showing himself the true Scholastic, with many "secundum quid's", many a "per se," as he hurries to his "Ergo" and his final conclusion. Like the old Interlocutor of the Black and White Minstrel Show, like some sort of Divine Interlocutor, caught forever between Black and White, between Mister Carbo and*

*Mister Hydrate—and that other Endman, Mister Bones—
saying endlessly On the One Hand, On the Other—the
Latin Utrum/An? or, as we used to have to do when we
were little boys in theology, even "Ho Men—Ho Day?" in
the original Greek.*

*"It is the Disputatio she wants!" I say to myself.
She wants the Question put, with all the Objections
listed and answered, in order, according to the old rules.
She asks Why? and How?; but if she is like the rest—
and I know them well—what she really wants to know
is When?, too. For I have found from experience, Next,
that those who ask How and Why of a moral decision
really demand its entire chronology. They want to
know when, precisely when it was decided, and are not
satisfied with anything else.*

*But, oh, Next—has anyone ever truly been able to
chronicle the history of a moral decision? To be able to
say precisely, "Here these norms were held, and there—
just at that point—after that—something else was held
with all the heart"?*

*It was not like that. I don't know how it is for others,
but for me it was more like a tide. I once watched a tidal
pool fill up, on the Maine coast. I was determined to
catch the moment of the tide's change, the exact moment
when the pool was filled and the instant it began to
empty. Aristotle almost lost his life doing it, he dived in
and almost drowned. I was no more successful. I kept
my eye on certain wisps of straw, a string of dried grass,
a gum wrapper. When they changed, I knew all changed.*

*But when that happened, it was already over. Some
grass was going one way, and some was going the other,
and in the end the gum wrapper was still going in the
wrong direction, but it had changed.*

7

Very well, then. You who are going to do nothing still ask the Question. I will try again. I will do the Disputatio *with you. I will defend. Not according to your medieval rules, however—"Ad Primum, Ad Secundum, Ad Tertium," full of "Ergos's" and "Sed Contra's"—but in my own way. Mine is mostly stories, yet it speaks to the question all the same, and it has its own argument, which can be followed at least as well as grass upon the waters. To me, it is a battle as bitter as any the gods of Homer set, the riddle with itself for an answer.*

I went back once, you know, to the old House of Theology. Nothing was left. The great tomes were gone, the smell of incense was gone, the choir stalls were gone, and the High Altar had been jack-hammered out. I followed the catena *mosaic in the marble up one corridor and down another. I found nothing. In the end all I found was that statue of the Sphinx we had, that antique brought over from ancient Egypt. There, at the intersection of classroom wing and Chapel wing, cartouche upon its shoulder, it still confronted the passer-by . . . all that black basalt was too heavy to move, apparently. I was awed; it still stared through me as it always had, its gaze fixed upon eternity.*

But, Next, I have a legitimate complaint. You have the advantage of me. For in the end, Asker, Questioner, Interrogator, you must know that it is like the Sphinx you come. It is like the Sphinx you come with your riddle, Riddle of the Ages, I standing there on slow feet at a fork in the way, knowing, both of us knowing, that in the end you will destroy me, will crush me to powder if I fail.

Well, then. Here goes.

The Breaking of
the String

MY FATHER was a streetcar man who wrote poetry between runs, while he was waiting at the Keating car barn on the north side of Pittsburgh. It was mostly about Galway Bay, or his home in Kilkenny, or his love for my mother, and his verse was full of borrowings from songs like "The Wearing of the Green" and "The Minstrel Boy." Some of his poems were written to be sung, and had as many as twenty or thirty verses, I think, which he would go singing in a stentorian voice through the house until my mother asked him to stop.

I would hold my ears, while the place shook, embarrassed and humiliated at the scene. He was always embarrassing me. At the Zoo, for instance, where he took me many times a year from when I was very little until I was eight or nine, we did something called "making the lions roar." Many people tease the lions, I know, but I have never seen anyone elicit the response that my father did. He would start out standing in front of the big, mangy-haired male—who was often half asleep—and yawn at him. Then my father would start to roar, with an enormous roar, ignoring the amused attention of the bystanders. I was embarrassed; my face would flush, and I would whisper, "Oh, Dad, *stop*," my sweaty little hand engulfed in his huge, calm paw. But he would go on, and if he was lucky, which was most times, the lion would become interested, or annoyed, or generally excited, and, finally, roar back at him, the King of Beasts feeling that his kingship of the entire place was being questioned. And the two of them would have a roaring duel, one mimicking the other, shouting the other down, making fun of the pretensions of the other, and one insulting the other, until the people came running from all over, and a crowd gathered, and the other animals got restive all over the Zoo, and until at last the animal keepers themselves would come running and put a stop to it.

Then my father would chuckle and saunter off, with me, to the equivalent of a few "Bravo's" from the crowd, and I was not quite so ashamed of him.

The trouble was, you see, that my father came from "the old country," which in his case meant Ireland. On my mother's side it meant Ireland, too, but Connemara, not Kilkenny, and from an early age I became dimly aware that an awful lot of our family's problems were due to the fact that our parents came from Ireland. At first I was heartbroken when I was told that I was not from there. I was an American, they told me, I was not Irish; but since both my parents were, they said, I was the next best thing. I cried at first, over not being Irish, going into the bathroom to weep in private. But after a while it began to seem to me that being from the old country was not perhaps the best thing in the world. In fact, I was well on the way toward my teens before I realized that our "old country" was not even the same as the "old countries" that other children spoke of. There was a clan of children at school, the Jurgevics, who spoke of an "old country" that was clearly not the same as ours; it was worse. I tried not to think of the Jurgevics; they all suffered from runny noses, and wore winter underwear through the entire year.

But perhaps I am wrong. My father was an unusual man; he would have been unusual no matter where he came from.

His favorite mode of building was with railroad ties. He built us a coal cellar—out of railroad ties. He said it was solid, and indeed it was. If a part of our hillside threatened to slip away after a rain, he would acquire from Pittsburgh Railways Company a supply of old creosoted track ties and have them delivered by a friend who had a truck. Then, usually on a Friday night, my father would come walking down our block on Dunlap Street with a huge, wooden, red-painted jack or hoist over his shoulders, of the sort used to put derailed streetcars back on the tracks. With this he could move anything, and all through the weekend, with ties and jack, he would push back into shape the very hill we lived on. The foundation shook, the house shook, and I shook, to see my mighty parent taming the earth itself. Inside, the process was only scaled down, and my mother was afraid to ask him to repair anything, for he was no good with anything smaller than two-by-fours and spikes.

He found an old cartridge belt from the First World

War somewhere, which he put on whenever he worked, to keep his rather substantial front from being a problem. His "War Belt" he called it. The family's first intimation that we were in for a window-rattling weekend was often his request for this. "Where is my War Belt?" he would bellow out to my mother, like some grand Celtic chieftain of old calling for his battle gear. I sometimes shook when he shouted that, too, for generally it was I who had misplaced it, playing with it, even though he had told me often enough that it was "no toy." To keep it away from me, I think, he left it in the top of his huge steamer trunk, along with such things as the deed to the house and his private papers; I was just strong enough, though, to lift the lid a crack and extract it.

But he was a joyful man, too, and very deeply religious. He had a deep and abiding belief that the sun danced with joy on Easter Sunday morning. A collection of black old Kodak negatives was kept in the sideboard, the darkest parts of which came in handy for viewing purposes. Every Easter as we walked to Mass there was much speculation about whether or not there would be clouds. Then, after breakfast—no matter what the weather conditions, really—there would be much fussing around in the buffet drawer for the film and we would all troop outside to see if the sun was dancing. When it was shining brightly, and I tried to look at it directly, it did indeed seem to me to be dancing—all over the sky. However, when I looked at it through the darkened film, it seemed to be quite unmoving. To my father, however, it always danced—cloud or no cloud, film or no film—and he danced with it.

I tried, I suppose, to be like him. But there was not much I could do. I could not make the lions roar. I could not move railroad ties around. I could not even see the sun dance, properly, the way my father did. I could not wear his War belt—when I fastened the buckle in front, the whole thing fell to my ankles.

I knew I was not like him, very much. But I was fond of him, I respected him, and we got along, at least until the fall in which it was time for me to enter First Grade. Then we had our fight. It was not about going to school, really, although everybody said it was. It was not at all about the thing it seemed to be about. It was about the old country, I am sure.

One day, late in the fall of the year in which I started school, my father took my two sisters and me to Boggs and Buhl's Department Store to buy overshoes. The girls got their galoshes—for that is what we call them in our family—first. Then I got mine. Only, mine were girls' galoshes.

I tried to tell him, "But these are *girls'*." As they were put on me I pointed to the wavy, unmistakably feminine line around the snap fasteners that rose high to the ankle in the latest women's fashion. "Dad," I shouted, "you're buying me *girls'* galoshes!"

My sisters looked at the monstrosities on my feet, the clerk looked at them, and I looked at them, and we all knew with perfect certitude that I was trying on girls' galoshes. My father looked at them, too, and saw all he needed to see.

"*Nonsense*, Child!" he roared. "They will keep your feet warm!"

I cried. I don't know what the clerk was doing selling girls' things to boys, but if either he or my sisters tried to object, their protests were lost in the wail of my sobs and the roar of my father's voice. "What a *mollycoddle*," he said. He had told us all again and again how our family had been present at the Battle of Clontarf—had, indeed, actually swung that battle, enabling the great Irish hero Brian Boru to drive the Danes into the sea. He looked at me there in the store and saw a puny offspring who would never be able to swing anything.

And I certainly didn't swing that day. I walked out of the store wearing girls' galoshes. And I walked to school the next day wearing girls' galoshes and keeping my feet warm. All the way up Ritchey Street, along Perrysville Avenue and Franklin Road, I hoped that the silly stupid things would drop off, would become invisible, would disappear, and that somehow—oh, *some*how—no one would notice them. But my fellow students were not from the old country. They knew, every one of them— even the Jurgevics knew—accurately and well what boys should wear and what girls should wear. I tried to take them off a block from school and carry them under my arm, but my sisters would not hear of it. My feet would get wet, they said, and I would catch cold, and they would be blamed. There was a fuss, and by the time I reached the cloakroom I had been subjected to ridicule that no child should ever have to undergo. That day, and every day that threatened to be the least bit damp, I wore them, and I was called a "pantywaist" and a "sissy." Even the girls were pained: look at what the kid's got on his feet.

I suffered, I tried to sneak out of the house without them. I dreaded the coming of snow. I got into fights. I socked John Jurgevic in the jaw while wearing my girls' galoshes. Word went around school: watch that little kid, he's tough for a boy who wears girls' galoshes.

But in the end I gave up. I ran home in my girls' galoshes and refused to go back. I had hated school all along anyway; the footgear debacle was all I needed.

No one understood. It was decided that I was "slow." Unbelievably, incredibly, for I really did not expect it, I was allowed to postpone my schooling for an entire year. A conference between my parents and the principal concluded that I was tied to my mother's apron strings. I had not seen enough of the world. I was frightened of everything.

What was needed, they agreed, was a program of introduction to the great world. It was begun: my father, during his off hours, took me on long walks (whether in or out of my galoshes, I know not). He looked at real estate, my hand in his; I worried about running into my happy, proud former classmates who wore the right things, and who had parents who knew what was coming off.

It was on one of these walks that the chasm between myself and my father began to be bridged; and the matter had little to do with overshoes. We were walking far out in the country, along Ivory Road, and I asked him how big was America? Was it as big as the other countries?

"*Child*," he responded, "why, Child, it's bigger than any of them. Your country could beat any five of the others put together. This is the richest country on earth."

He walked along, his thoughts doubtless returning to land values. But my little mind had been expanded by a new fact. It was, possibly, the first time I ever really believed anything he said; and it was, possibly the first time he ever listened to me.

And with that, things began to change.

After that I refused to remain in the kitchen with my

sisters on Sunday afternoons at four o'clock when Father Coughlin was on the radio. It was tempting ruin, I knew, to come out, for my father did not wish to be disturbed. He sat the whole hour with his head an inch away from the old Majestic so as not to miss a single word while the Radio Priest, speaking from the National Shrine of the Little Flower, at Royal Oak, Michigan, thundered forth about the Just Annual Living Wage, the Soldiers' Bonus Bill, the Gold Standard, and someone called the International Bankers. But I stayed quiet for the hour, unnoticed, and a thrill ran up and down my spine and out to my fingers and toes each time the great voice pounded out his promise to "Drive the money-changers out of the Temple of America!"

Somewhere in there I got all excited about the International Bankers. I don't know what became of my girls' galoshes. I had new problems. For all during the Thirties, you see, my father and I hammered out our Foreign Policy. Beginning at the age of eight or nine, I walked around with the entire weight of America's Foreign Policy upon my head.

We argued. He began to speak to me as if I were Franklin Delano Roosevelt's Secretary of War, as if I had the ear of the President the way Cordell Hull did. We would walk down Perrysville Avenue shouting at one another. He would call me—standing in for all my fellow Americans—a "Yankee Sap." He blamed me for being taken in by Henry Wallace's Farm Plan. I insisted that I was not, that I saw through it. He said Harry Hopkins should be watched. I said I had been watching him.

I remember being very angry with Bernard Mannes Baruch. I don't know why. Other kids didn't know his last name; they were collecting baseball cards. But I knew his middle name, and despised him. I walked around the house repeating "Bernard Mannes Baruch" the way Father Coughlin did, and telling my sisters about the National Debt.

I became an Isolationist, and rattled off the names of Borah, Nye, and Fish. In the first year of High School, I got up in front of my History class and delivered a plea against Roosevelt's decision to give fifty over-age destroyers to England. I called the Jurgevics "Yankee Saps" that day, but no one else in the room agreed with me. They were all tools of England. I shouted at them like Father Coughlin would. And I went home and decided to become a priest to save the world from the International Bankers, who were behind everything.

As I grew older, we stopped going to the Zoo, and went instead to Allegheny County Municipal Airport to see the planes. A child of my time, I was able to explain things to my father. I would stand up on the railing to get a better look, telling him of the difference between Douglases and Boeings. He was amazed. He asked me, at an air show, what weight bombers could carry, and how far they could carry it. I was able to give him reliable answers, for I read the syndicated columns of Major Al Williams, a latter-day Billy Mitchell, and relayed to my Father what I had learned there. I spoke of the Hamilton Variable-Pitch Propeller, and of the superiority of the inverted, liquid-cooled engine for fighter planes. Al Williams had been to Germany and had seen the Luftwaffe in practice.

But my father was more worried about the Japanese. He remembered the Russo-Japanese War in the year 1904, the year in which he came to America. "You think the Japs are going to wait for you, Child!" he would bel-

low at me, making my knees give a little. "Oh, ye Yankee
Saps! The Japs aren't going to wait for you! They're
going to *bum* you." He always pronounced it that way
when he was excited. "They're going to *bum* you first,
just like they did to the Russians at Port Arthur in 1904!"

I paid little attention; he was always talking about the
Boer War, or the Spanish-American War, or the Russo-
Japanese War. He lived, more or less, at the turn of the
century. I was sick of hearing about Port Arthur. I got
tired of being blamed for mistakes that I had not made,
and I complained, on behalf of myself and my entire nation. But he never heard that. And soon we would be off
again, on the Boer War, the Spanish-American War, and
the rest of it. But always he came back to the Japanese;
the Jap, he said, was going to hit me first.

I thought of the sun dancing, and the ridiculous mistake in the department store which had made me, always,
one year older than I should be. And I put it with Roaring at Lions.

One of the last things we did together was, I think, to
plant grass. We were always planting grass. I don't know
what happened to the stuff we had planted before, unless
we watered it too much, but every year as I moved
on to High School the lawn seemed to require new sod.
My father's solution to the problem was typical of him.
He would go off down the hillside to find a plot of green-
ery. He would shovel loose a supply of clumps, then pile
them high—always too high—on the old wheelbarrow.
My job came in when the wheel got stuck. There was a
rope tied to the front. I pulled up, the wheel came un-
stuck, and we would groan on toward home. The scene
always reminded me of something out of Aesop's Fables,
but years later, on Ordination Day, as he kissed my hands,

it was hauling sod together that my father remembered most.

One Sunday afternoon in High School, I was lying on my bed fighting a cold. My Mother called up to me, Where was Pearl Harbor? It had been bombed. I rushed downstairs, to see my father pointing to it on the globe. "The Jap has hit you," he said.

I looked at him with amazement. That Irish potato farmer, that singing streetcar man, that writer of bad verse and roarer at lions had all along known more than many a general, and many an admiral, who did not even know the way to plant sod.

He never boasted of it, never once claimed that he had said it all along. He asked me how old I was. And when I answered, his eyes took on a more worried look behind the old dime-store glasses.

I never went to war. When my time came I entered the seminary. I had wanted to be a priest since Father Coughlin and maybe even before, and I still wanted to be one in 1943—though not, I think, because of the International Bankers. I have often worried that I was a Draft Dodger. I still do, though it may seem ridiculous. I still worry that I acted wrongly; but I think no, on balance.

My father died not quite ten years ago. For a long time I could not bring myself to go through the contents of his trunk. Then, last week, for reasons of business, I went over to it and lifted the lid once again. There, on top, was the old War Belt. What I expected to find underneath was deeds and titles and rent receipts, but I was surprised; it was mostly packet upon packet of his poems, all carefully saved and tied together with strings.

I hesitated, for I was not sure what he would want. But finally I opened one; and everything came dancing and singing and shouting back at me. I forgot what I had come for, and read them all.

*　*　*　*　*

Father, forgive the breaking of the string. Saintly Father, Lion-Tamer, Old Earth-Shaker. Nine years have passed since these songs rattled the windows, and still I am the one year older. I bear your marks.

I see here, in the massive cross-ties of your verse, Trestle-Builder, that you loved me, and had huge hopes.

I have nothing to report. There is much less thunder now. Your War Belt is at peace. I have not made the earth to shake. I wish I could say that the sun does dance, but I cannot.

No. It is only me, Proud Parent. And I do not make the lions roar.

⚱ RIGHT-ANGLE BEND

One more thing, my friend, before I leave the streetcar man behind. There was the astronomer, too. He speaks to the question.

The great three-domed observatory of Doctor John A. Brashear—Allegheny Observatory, fourth-largest in the world—dominated our horizon. He was the one who taught us never to look directly at the sun.

He worked all through the night, and at dawn, my father would pick him up on the last returning trolley of the night shift, holding the car for him, even, if he was late. The two men became fast friends. I can guess how it worked: Doctor Brashear laughing at my father's wonderful stories, my father asking the great astronomer if he ever saw any angels through his telescope. One ques-

tion I know he asked the old scientist was about eternity; he often asked him about the next life, and whether or not Doctor Brashear had any worries about that. "—I asked him—Doctor Brashear is not a Catholic—if he believed in Heaven or Hell, or thought much about death. And do you know what he said? He said to me, 'I have loved the stars too fondly to have any fear of the night.' Now, what do you suppose he meant by that?"

I remember Doctor Brashear distinctly. We were invited over often to look through one of the telescopes. My sister would go skipping along ahead, reciting her astronomy: "Draco, the Dragon—Boetes, the Hunter— Ursa, the Bear . . ." And then as we mounted Observatory Hill she would read out the names sculpted along the top of the building: "Kepler . . . Galileo . . . Langley . . . Tycho Brahe."

For a child—for anyone—to be inside even the smallest of the great domes, the one the public was allowed into, was marvelous. The floor moved. Zacheus Daniels, Doctor Brashear's aged assistant, would go over to the brick wall and pull on a coil of rope. There would be a low, long roar, and we would move up toward the telescope— you could see the floor rise past brick row after brick row. Mister Daniels pulled on another rope—another roar, and the dome moved toward where we were going to look. Then, wonder of wonders, he pulled on another rope, and the great dome itself actually opened, and you could see out into the night sky. The telescope moved easily, to the touch of a small cord held in Doctor Brashear's hand.

I got to know the old man for a specific reason: I was too small to look through his telescope. I was a nuisance. After the floor was raised, the dome rotated, the aperture opened, everyone else could see, and the line of viewers took their turn. But then it came to me, whose head was a foot beneath the end of the telescope. "Ahh—the little fellow!" Doctor Brashear would say. "Get him his elbow! —Get the right-angle bend!" Zacheus Daniel would fix in a right-angled, elbowed eyepiece that brought things down to me ("There you are, Sir!"), and I would look through the entire gigantic telescope by myself. While the others waited and talked, I looked at the mountains of the moon.

I would try to find in my eyepiece what it was they were talking about—the great craters of Clavius, Plato, Copernicus, and the dark seas, Mare Imbrium, the Sea of Serenity, the Sea of Storms—until my sister would shout, right into my ear: "Betelgeuse! Betelgeuse! He's going to look at Betelgeuse!" to get me away from it, so that Doctor Brashear would unfasten my right-angle lens and everyone else would be able to see what was next.

Doctor Brashear died years later, when I was in the seminary. One morning at dawn my father waited for him, held the car as long as he could, then had to move on.

It came as a beautiful surprise, though, that he had chosen for his epitaph the lines he had spoken to my father:

> *I have loved the stars too fondly*
> *To have any fear of the night.*

I can imagine my father putting on his glasses, reading slowly the words inscribed into the wall at the base of the telescope, repeating them word for word; then thinking for a moment, saying to no one in particular, "Now, what do you suppose he meant by that?"

♆ SIGN . . . . . .

There—wisps of straw at least, going one way. Never mind the gum wrapper.

You see how gradual some things are, they move considerably one way before ever starting back the other. There are slack tides. God breathes over all deeps, yours, mine, whoever we are; turbulence comes soon enough.

But, Semblable, *you demand a sign. There are few; we are lucky to get even such signs as Jonah, three days in the belly of a whale, then tossed up upon the beach.*

Question: Was even Jonah afraid of that beach? That he would be left forever there, to perish on the shore?

The Battle of Boiling Water

W E H A D A Depression Plant right in the middle of our dining room table: a piece of Pennsylvania coal, planted as though it were a living thing, in a strange ground made up of chemicals and dyes, specially chosen and carefully arranged upon a platter of cut glass. The Depression Plant seemed to be growing; it was shaped like a mountain, and I used to spend hours watching sick little forests of purple and green and white crystals climb its small, alpine valleys, and gradually conceal the mass of black on which they grew.

Outside, the Bonus Army was getting ready to march on Washington. I knew all about it. All through that dark Pittsburgh winter, unemployed men had been coming to our kitchen door asking for coffee or cigarettes or shoes, and I would stare out at them from behind my mother, and sometimes talk to them. I saw where they lived, too, when we went to Old Saint Patrick's Church, once a month, for the Lourdes Novena. The church was right next to the railroad, near the freight yards of the Union Depot, and that was where the men lived, in Shantytown. Going past Shantytown was the most exciting part of the trip to the Lourdes Novena. My father tried to march us past it briskly in a military formation but I would always hang back, for I wanted to see it. I would ask questions; but he would only say, angrily, that something was rotten with America, or that Andy Mellon should be taken out and shot; then he would hurry me on, to the Novena.

I liked the inside of Old Saint Patrick's Church, for it was not really a church at all. Half of it, all down one side, was given over to a full-sized model or replica of the grotto in Lourdes, France, where Our Lady of the Immaculate Conception had appeared nine times in a row to a shepherd girl named Bernadette Soubirous. I was captivated and filled with delight that anyone would think of bringing a thing like that in from outside and putting it in a church; that was better than the shanties, even.

The man who had done it was Father Cox. He was not as good as Father Coughlin, but almost. He had brought stones from the very spot in France where Our Lady had stood, and the men from Shantytown had come, being out of work, and had built the huge shrine for him. It had everything—candles, and vigil lights, and even sheep. There was ivy all up and down the rocks of the grotto; then there was Bernadette, kneeling, beside a spring of real water; and, finally, there was our Blessed

Lady, high up above everything, with roses on her feet. There were crutches and canes and medical braces as well, left there by people who had been cured by the Lourdes water, and some of the crutches, I knew, were from the men wounded in the war.

The service ended with the singing of the Lourdes Hymn, *"Ave, Ave, Ave Maria,"* which I could sing very well, and which I sang very loudly, for I wanted to be like Father Cox and Father Coughlin; I wanted to grow up and be a priest and help lead the men.

But, to tell the truth, I was not happy as I sang. I had done something wrong, you see. I had committed a sin. That was not too bad, perhaps; I knew from Catechism class that every human being was guilty of some sin and needed to be forgiven. But that was the whole point. My particular failure had been so private, and so personal, and so embarrassing that I could not bring myself to talk about it, even in the Confessional. I went up to Confession one Saturday afternoon at my home church and waited in line; and when my time came I told all my faults but that one humiliating thing. When the priest asked, "Is that all, Son?" I lied; I said, "Yes." And when it was over I had held back a sin in Confession, something I had heard that other people did, but something I had never, never in my life thought I would be capable of.

And the following week it wasn't any easier, for now I really had something difficult to mention; at first I'd only had the thing that I had done by myself in the bedroom, but now I had held back a sin in Confession. I had received a Sacrament unworthily. I had committed, therefore, what the Catechism called a Sacrilege: I had

lied to God. And how could I ever manage to tell that
to anybody?

How had I gotten myself into such a state? It is a long,
painful story.

There was a very attractive girl at school named Jean
Marie Mangan. She was the brightest girl in class, and I
was the brightest boy. I remember telling my sister once,
in a flush of honesty, that there was a girl just like her at
school. I liked Jean Marie Mangan—no, I loved her—
but she was the enemy; she competed with me for every
prize. We spent years "trapping" one another in recitation lines; she would go up in Mathematics, and I would
go down; but then I would go up in Geography, and
she would go down; and we both pointedly ignored one
another, on the way up and on the way down.

All the same, I loved her, and carried everywhere within me her double: a Jean Marie Mangan faithful in every
detail of walk and word and gesture, but one much more
approachable, who let herself be talked to. And I talked
to her, in a far more kind and gentlemanly way than I
ever did to the real one.

In public, however, our rivalry was intense. We pointedly ignored one another on the way to school, too; even
when we happened to drop into Isaly's Dairy Store together, only disparaging comments were exchanged.

Not everyone was fooled, however. A pimply-faced
young man behind Isaly's ice cream counter saw everything. He knew; oh, he knew, all right; he knew everything. He was a Protestant, and much older than I. He
teased me about being a Roman Catholic; it was from
his lips I first heard of "The Battle of Boiling Water."
He meant the famous Battle of the River Boyne, in Ire-

land, of course, where King James II was defeated by William of Orange, but neither of us knew that.

> "Ten thousand Micks
> Lost their necks . . . "

he would sing to me as he worked

> " . . . At the *Battle of Boiling Water!*"

It was a warfare we carried on. I could not get away from him; whenever he saw me coming, he was always free. I would order my ice-cream cone and wait with my nickel on the counter, but it took him forever. And after he got done singing "The Battle of Boiling Water," he eventually got around to the subject of girls.

Today I realize that with that Emperor of Ice Cream it was a labor of love; that he spent most of the day sculpting and molding enormous, pointed, uproariously phallic cones for the parochial school children of Pittsburgh. He was a teacher; he educated while he worked; a stream of under-breath mutterings of every kind of obscenity explained all man needed to know. And the last words he always said to me as he handed me my oversized, pinnacled cone, the words I could always clearly hear, were, "Ooooooh—he *played* with it!"

I hated his talk, but I loved ice cream, and as long as I had the money to spend, we fought each time the Battle of the Boyne. Which I now know I lost.

One Thursday, after the Protestant forces had vanquished for the thousandth time the last of the Catholic Stuarts in that miserable, hateful old battle, I found myself singing again in the weekly choir practice. Jean Mangan and I competed at this, too. We stood directly across the aisle from one another, singing very hard. That day we were practicing a hymn called "Peace, It Is I!," a song such as a boy would like, for it was full of shipwrecks, tempests, billows, and a strange, impossible monster called the Whale of Euroclydon. "Whale of Euroclydon," we sang, "be thou at rest," not knowing what it was we were singing about. I sang it better than anyone, for I was the only one who could really pronounce the word. I was the one who got us past "Euroclydon," and I was very proud. But as I sang that day before the Lord my God the hymn "Peace, It Is I!" and appeared to gaze most intently at the Tabernacle upon the altar, I knew very well that my eyes were really only upon the lovely face and body of Jean Marie Mangan, and I was hoping that she heard.

Something had to be done. I recalled the things that had been said to me. The young man at Isaly's had congratulated me openly upon her again and again; he had suggested that riotous things must have already taken place or, if they had not, were vastly overdue. He was a fool, of course, and yet I knew that a fight was building up; that sooner or later that fight must be fought; and that if I did not win it, I would never be a priest.

What ridicule would I have endured had he really known the truth? For the truth was that for many weeks now, months even, I had longed to run away and leave Pittsburgh forever, in the company of Jean Marie Mangan, and did so, in my imagination, many times a day. On each trip to the grocery I escaped with her to those strange places that I knew so much about: to the banks of the Indus and the Oxus; to the rock-carved city of Petra, in the desert; then far, far beyond, to the Upper Kingdom of old Egypt, past the Six Great Cataracts, even to the Sources of the Nile. But always, always, most of all, last of all, to fabled Samarkand. We rode on Bactrian camels, which I knew from Geography were the ones with two humps, and I defended her from all dangers, including, even, sometimes, in some rather unusual circumstances, the Whale of Euroclydon.

And yet who was really the fool? For I loved the world, and I loved Jean Mangan; but I knew that I could never really go to Samarkand with her, or anyplace, if I was to become a priest.

Something did have to be done, therefore; and I wondered, as I sang, what I was to do.

When I got home I still had not thought of a solution, so I went down into the cellar, for I wanted to think, and that was where I thought.

There were books down there—discarded, extra books, too large or too worn to be kept in the living room upstairs. There were books on fishing, and mountain climbing, and gardening, in among some old *National Geographic* magazines. My sea books were there, too, with splendid color pictures of H.M.S. *Repulse* and H.M.S. *Renown* firing broadside off Gibraltar, and of S.S. *Orantes* passing the Seven Sisters. But the book I liked most of all, and the one that always set me thinking best, was *The Wonder Book of the World*. It was large and beautifully bound, with leather that had come from Morocco, my father said; its cover had a nautical compass embossed upon it in the center, with a boy riding a dolphin through the waves out toward the edge. I often wondered how the boy stayed on, and what it must be like to glide from wave to wave, and to plunge into the green depths, and whether or not he could breathe underwater. Once when I was swimming at North Park I tried it; dunked my head under the water and opened my eyes. Everything was green and blue, and all sounds became squeals as I felt the pressure of depth. I tried swallowing, without opening my mouth; but the strange, orgasmic squeak that I heard surprised me, and I surfaced at once. All the same, I loved the big book, and was fond of turning its pages, thinking of what I would be when I grew up.

Before I had even gotten to the Great Pyramids of Cheops that day, I knew what I should do.

I went up to my bedroom and took down my model of H.M.S. *Agamemnon*, the pride of the Royal Navy, from my dresser, and put it on the mantel. Then I found a statue of Our Blessed Lady, and a box of Mother's Oats, which was round and strong and could serve as a hidden base. I emptied the cereal into a bowl, and stood the statue of Our Lady upon the box, and surrounded it with a cloth, spraying it with paint; and soon I had my own grotto complete with tiny crutches, even, made from match sticks. Beside it all I placed a bottle of Lourdes water from Old Saint Patrick's Church, and, as I lit the vigil light in front of it, made a vow to Our Blessed Lady that I would become a priest, and would help to save the world.

For a whole week I did not think of Jean Mangan— or at least did not go on any imaginary voyages with her, though it was hard keeping her out of trips to the Karakorams, or to the Steppes of Central Asia. All through the week I read with growing excitement what Father Cox had to say about the Soldiers' Bonus and the impending march on Washington. I even returned the taunts of the young man at Isaly's, secure in the knowledge of my secret grotto (whence all my strength came). I played ball on Dunlap Street with coarse companions and, at certain very strategic moments of the day, went home to light the vigil light to renew my consecration. And yet, by the end of the week I had fallen, in the manner I have described.

After that, life became very difficult. I was, essentially, waiting to go to Confession. The thing to do was to confess my failure as quickly as possible, and to start over.

But when Saturday came and I found that, because of one pitiful small detail in the matter, I could not bring myself to confess it, everything became awful.

The days were all right. For one thing, I was good at baseball as it was played in the streets. I was generally chosen first, to bat fourth and to be "clean-up" man. I would stand at the manhole cover we used for home-plate, and hit the ball over the head of the last little child who was "backing up" away down the block, and who was supposed to keep the ball from rolling into the Ritchey Street sewer; and while he chased it I would stride triumphantly around the bases, to the admiration of my companions, all but forgetting that I had held back a sin in Confession.

But the nights were different. For then I had to go home and face my problem with God, alone; and my God was a fierce God.

I had the soundest theological authority for believing that because I had committed what was called a Mortal Sin, and then had gone on to commit yet another, more serious sin of Sacrilege, I had left Him no choice. He would rightly—indeed, could in no way do otherwise and truly be God—cast me into eternal damnation. And it was not just a case of what the Catechism said, either, or certain great theologians; the New Testament itself was uncompromising on such things: "Depart from me, ye cursed," it said, "into everlasting fire," and talked of the "exterior darkness," where there was weeping and gnashing of teeth. It said it over and over in different ways. It spoke of an unquenchable fire and an unquenchable thirst; and it seemed to me that whenever I went to the Bible for help, it always fell open at such places.

And yet I did not want to be judged on any weaker grounds.

As the night wore on I could not fall asleep, for I was beginning to be conscious of what would happen if I should die during the night. Here was a whole new horror which had not occurred to me before. I began to not want to fall asleep.

I listened to my heart. It was beating faithfully; indeed, it seemed to be the one faithful thing I had under the circumstances, and so I talked to it in the darkness. I became wonderfully aware of how all life was really only one heartbeat away from nothing. And so I urged my heart on; and I remember promising it that if it would do its share and get us both safely into the morning, I would do the rest; I would get up and go to Confession and clear the whole thing up, so that I and my body and my conscience and my heart could all live merrily together and at peace once again.

Only when morning came, and the sun shone, and the light of day made things seem not quite so bad, I reneged, and went to school, and played ball, and so guaranteed that I would face my problems once more in the same old way, on a bed of pain, and in the darkness of the night.

I began not to be able to put up with it, falling into fitful periods of sleep that was not sleep, half dreaming, half worrying. I seemed far out at sea, like that boy on a dolphin, the last, lonely, clanging bell that marked any-thing having been left far behind; and it was in this mel-ancholy seascape of long, deep ocean swells, of parting and of closing mists, of muffled distances and of the cries of unknown sea birds, that I first spied or sensed or felt that strange creature from the Antipodes: the whale, my own special whale, Euroclydon, that has never left me. "Whale of Euroclydon, be thou at rest," I said weakly, hopelessly. Oh, I did not see him, I knew that; I more heard him, or felt him, along the region of the heart; but I knew what he was like. I felt that his arrival was long overdue; I felt, even, relieved—that it was about time we should be introduced.

I tried to pray. I lit the vigil light in front of Our Lady's statue, but the flickering wick only cast more shadows into the room, and the pathetic little grotto only reminded me of all my previous foolishnesses, my vain hopes and wild ambitions, and so I put the flame out. And in the dark that followed, I tried singing. "Whale of Euroclydon," I sang, "be thou at rest," but softly, so that he might hear, and no one else.

I began to argue. Finally, I could take it no more. I realized perfectly well that a person in the state of sin had no right to pray to God, that the only prayers of his that had a chance of being answered were those which asked for a release from that state, and these I could not or would not utter. I began to feel, vaguely, put upon, for I knew that boys were not supposed to undergo such things; my friends in the street obviously did not. And so I began to argue with Him; what kind of God was it that let a person get into something like this? What kind of God did He think He was anyway? And what about crip-pled children? If He was so good, how did it happen that everything was so all screwed up? Why did everything need saving anyway?

Then I would become frightened and think about what I had said. I had presumed to question my Maker: I would be damned now more than before, if that was possible. I turned over fiercely in my bed and listened to the old house creak; no one else, apparently, was having any trouble. And I went to sleep, only to dream of that creature nine fathoms deep underneath the keel, from the land of mist and snow. It was Euroclydon; for, make no mistake, he was out there somewhere, only he was waiting; he had all the time in the world, a special whale for those who had lied to God; and I would wake up seeing that baleful eye, and almost shouting. But no: the grotto was still there, and H.M.S. *Agamemnon* as well, outlined by the light from the streetlamp. And so I swung, a ridiculous young boy, from Jonah to Job, and from Job back to Jonah again; and I still don't understand what business I had with any of it.

And so, night after night, I wrestled with God—or rather with the idea of Him, for I was beginning to think He no longer existed. My fight was now no longer with flesh and blood; it was no longer about Jean Mangan, even. I began to doubt: no god would be that cruel. The books in Carnegie Library were true, then, that said there wasn't any, and that my Faith was wrong. And that made the fellow at Isaly's probably right about the Battle of Boiling Water. . . . At last, I hoped that my God would go away, and take his church, and his whale, and his priesthood with him.

I cannot say that God came to me in the whirlwind, or that He spoke to me, or that He even helped me at all.

But one Friday evening in May, after a satisfactory afternoon of hitting the ball very far down Ruggles Street
again and again, I came home determined to do something about my problem. I ate supper, and read the papers to see what was going on with the world and with
the men of the Bonus Army; then I went down to the
cellar to think. I went over to the books and glanced
through one about the Knights of the Round Table, and
another on Schliemann's discovery of the site of ancient
Troy. I spent the rest of the hour paging through one
of my mountain-climbing books, about the Himalayas.

But I was procrastinating, for the book I wanted was
called *The Catechism of Christian Doctrine*; it was full
of questions and answers having to do with moral problems, and I was well acquainted with it.

I had a thought, you see. I wanted to check and make
absolutely sure that the first thing I had done was really
a Mortal Sin after all. There were conditions for this
sort of thing, I knew, and it was just possible that I had
not fulfilled them, that what I had done was to be classed
only as a Venial Sin. If that was true, then I had not held
back anything serious in Confession, either; and I had
not lied to God. If that was the case, I was free, free to
enjoy life again.

My mother called down to me: what was I doing down
there? Shouldn't I be going to bed? I said that I would
soon, and would remember to shut the light out after me.
She went to put my younger brother to bed, and I found
the book.

There were three conditions necessary for the commis-
sion of a Mortal Sin, the kind of sin that cut a person
off from God, the book said. First, the failure had to in-
volve a grievous matter. I read on for quite a while, but

the more I read, the more it was clear that sex was always grievous, and that if you failed in this respect, which was my case, there could be no help from condition number one.

"Sufficient Reflection" was condition number two. I reflected upon whether I had reflected. And I decided that I had. I wished that I had not; I wished that I had just gone on and done it without thinking.

Number three appeared the only hope left to me; the last thing required was "Full Consent of the Will." There were definitions of Consent from Saint Thomas Aquinas, and some paragraphs on Freedom by theologians with Spanish-sounding names. But when I got finished with it all, I was no better off than if I had gone up to my bedroom and tried to sleep. I was damned in the cellar as well as in my room. I had still lied to God; only now I was sure of it.

How ridiculous it all was. I knew that I should laugh, but I felt like crying. I put the book back in its dusty place next to the travel volumes, and turned to leave; but as I did so, something strange caught my attention, off in the shadow of the shelves. I was startled; from its shape I did not know what it might be. I went over cautiously to investigate it, and found that it was the old Depression Plant, still sitting in its dish, but protected by newspapers and placed carefully in the center of a bushel basket. Someone had grown tired of seeing it on the dining-room table, and had put it down there preparatory to throwing it out.

I looked at it. It was growing away there in the dark, without light or air or even water, with nothing but itself to feed on; it seemed poisonous and hateful, and yet I knew that I was looking into a mirror. What a sublime joke I had become. From the brightest boy in the class, to my unreal relationship with Jean Mangan, to the fellow at Isaly's, to the ridiculous sin I had committed; and now to this: down in the cellar with the Depression Plant, arguing with Saint Thomas Aquinas about everlasting life, and worrying about whales.

I was too much of something for my own good. I was too much of everything, maybe. I thought too much. I read too much. I daydreamed, and worried about God too much. And in my plan for the salvation of the world, I was concerned with many things that any adult could have told me are better left alone. ("For who can draw out Leviathan with a hook?" I want to shout back, now, to that strange theologian of a boy. "And Euroclydon," I want to ask, "shalt thou play with him as with a bird, and catch him in thy nets?")

I shut the light off, went up to bed, and fell asleep.

The next day being Saturday, I got myself cleaned up and went to church. I knelt at the altar rail to ask for courage; then I joined the long line of sinners waiting to be forgiven. Most of them were little children, younger than I, for I had strategically chosen to go to their Confessor, old Father O'Connor, who was almost too deaf to hear, and too distant to understand. The line slowly bumped its way toward salvation past a steam radiator, making the tinny covering sound out from time to time through the old church; and finally it was my turn.

No dog sick in a corner ever vomited up more violently than I confessed my sins that time. I coughed up my days and ways fiercely, determinedly, in detail, gasping for air between sins to tell everything, everything, so that what I had gone through I would never have to go through again. My hands fastened themselves to the top of the kneeler so that I would not run away, and I told each failure, starting with the bedroom, to the holding back in the Confessional, to the many secret thoughts I had had, and ending finally with the crowning sin of disbelief, of having doubted the existence of God.

And old Father O'Connor, who was too distracted to understand the enormity of my guilt, and too concerned with his own special themes to give any thought to mine, waited impatiently for me to be silent. At last I was done, and then he spoke. He talked at some length against going to movies on Sunday; he gave me a light penance, and then he said the words of Absolution. I was free.

I cannot now say what I then felt: lions, harts, and leaping does could not have bounded forth from that confining place with more joy than I did. I burst out into the day, and saw that it was afternoon. A gentle May mist was falling, nourishing the lilac trees and honey-suckled lawns of Franklin Road; I was astonished at how lovely rain smelled; it had been raining on the way up, too, but I had not noticed. I remember stopping on the wooden steps leading down from the side door of the church. The railing was of course wet with rain; I went over to it and pounded it with my fist, glorying that it was real and that I could enjoy it. And later on, when the sun did shine, I almost could not stand the beauty of the day. I would go to Holy Communion in the morning with everyone else, and eternity held no fears for me.

I stopped at the newspaper stand on the corner of Perrysville Avenue and East Street: there were front-page pictures of the Pittsburgh contingent of the Bonus Army standing on boxcars in the nation's capital, and pictures of tombstones with "Andy Mellon" written on them; and there was the news that Father Coughlin had sent the men a check for $5,000, stipulating only that they not allow the virus of International Communism to penetrate their ranks.

I hurried home, for on Saturdays we had a genuine ballgame on the sand lot. I rounded the top of Ritchey Street full of anticipation, and triumph, and a pride that I had not felt for a long time.

And there, coming up Ritchey Street on the opposite sidewalk, was Jean Marie Mangan. She was on her way to Confession. Her knees shone whitely and prettily against the edge of her dress as she climbed the hill. What sins could she possibly have to tell?

For a moment I did not know what to do; then I shouted across the rectangular old limestone cobblestones of Ritchey Street a loud and respectful "Hello." It was the closest I ever came to saying what I thought.

For a while it seemed that my God was marching on, with the Bonus Army, under our very windows. But within a few days the names of Douglas MacArthur and Dwight Eisenhower became famous; they had routed the men with cavalry and tanks in Washington. The men came streaming home along the railroad tracks to Johnstown and Ambridge and Aliquippa, and I did not know what to think. I found myself standing on the sand lot, looking out over the rooftops of Pittsburgh, wondering about it, and about all things.

I had pretty much made up my mind to go to Samarkand alone, but I had not solved everything. I thought and thought, throughout the summer, about what had happened. I thought about Pittsburgh and Shantytown, and the men, and Father Cox, and Old Saint Patrick's Church, and the Grotto of Our Lady of Lourdes. But the more I thought, the more it only seemed clear to me that there were people in Pittsburgh who believed that Our Lady of Lourdes wanted Andy Mellon taken out and shot. And that finished it; I couldn't get past that, for it made me smile even though I didn't want to. And that's the way it ended, with a smile and a shake of the head toward Shantytown.

But it is really not over yet. It is years later, and I still have not solved anything. I think of a boy on a dolphin, years ago, riding out toward the edges of a dangerous sea. And I want to warn him, to shout something back at him across the years. "Behold Euroclydon," I want to say; "for he makes the deep sea to boil, and he leaves a path in the water shining after him. But there is no power on earth that can hold him. Small rider, he has broken all our nets."

☟ KAMIKAZE . . . . .

During the early years of this century, Japanese youths fell mightily in love with American baseball—beisbol, I believe they call it. They had the same heroes we had; I don't know whether they collected bubble-gum cards with Ducky Medwick, Grover Cleveland Alexander, or Van Lingel Mungo, the way we did, but they had the same heroes, for the Yankees and other teams traveled to Japan, and the visiting behemoths—Babe Ruth, Lou Gehrig, and the rest—knocked the ball out of the park to stupendous ovations.

The century moved on, and Japan struck against the West—for everything, all the way back to Perry's flagship in the bay and those miniature trains he set loose over the countryside. The young boys who learned baseball went on to learn something else. And during the bomb-

*ing of Pearl Harbor, American radio operators inter-
cepted Japanese pilot after Japanese pilot, each one
shouting, "To Hell with Babe Ruth! To Hell with Babe
Ruth!"*

*When I first heard that, I was uncomfortable, embar-
rassed. I understood perfectly: I am flying, white scarf
fluttering around my neck, goggles shining in the sun,
all honor to the Divine Wind as I line my bombs up
shouting over and over, in the language of the foreigner,
"To Hell with Babe Ruth! To Hell with Babe Ruth!"*

Four Ways
of Computing
Midnight

"JUDAS PRIEST!" said Billy Simmonds, hanging on
to the back of the cattle truck and kicking his cowboy
boots excitedly, *"Ju-das-K-Priest!"* Every time the truck
rounded a bend and gave us a glimpse of where we were
going, he repeated it: *"Judas Priest!"* he would say, darting a wild look at me, and then he would say, *"Judas
Priest!"* again.

I smiled, as I often did when he talked like that, and I
looked away, off into the distance, for I was excited, too.
All twenty of us on the back of the truck were joyful, for
it was transporting us past fields of ripening corn and
wheat to the one place we wanted to be: the Novitiate of
the Holy Cross, in Rolling Prairie, Indiana.

It was a strange time, however, for a group of young

men to be on a truck bound for anything other than military service, for the year was 1944. We were aware of the strangeness, of course, and most of us felt uncomfortable in our black clerical suits.

My black suit, at least, felt very uncomfortable on me. I had grown up fascinated with the world of the Thirties, preparing itself for war. I spent my childhood on the North Side of Pittsburgh dreaming about becoming a fighter pilot. I covered my schoolbooks with drawings of Spitfires and Hurricanes and Messerschmitts, and with Stukas dive-bombing tanks. With my friends in the streets, I collected the "War Cards" that came with bubble gum. We would divide up the gum as we came out of what we called "the Jew store" on Perrysville Avenue and then look feverishly at scenes of war in places like China and Spain and Ethiopia. We played games with the cards, flipping them against walls and people's front steps and talking about what we wanted to be when we grew up. I let everyone else talk, for I wanted to be the grandest thing of all. And when they were finished and asked me what I wanted to be, I said I would be a Navy fighter pilot, who took off from catapults over the waves and had to land his plane on the deck of the carrier, which was the size of a football field but which looked from the air no larger than a postage stamp in the ocean. Then everybody else would say, "Wow!" and for a while they wanted to be that, too.

And yet, as I grew older, I became somehow blessed with what was known as a Vocation. A Vocation was something that came quietly, for it was really the voice of God. It called you when you were young, to give your life to God in His priesthood. You heard it in the strangest places—when you were playing in the streets, or talking with friends, or turning over at night in your bed. I talked with my Confessor about it in the darkened Confessional up in Nativity Church on Saturday afternoons— Father Hanlon. I explained things to him over and over, trying to settle it, trying, in a way, to get rid of it, but trying to be fair: for I knew—every Catholic boy knew— that a Vocation was a wonderful thing, undoubtedly the most wonderful thing in all the world; to neglect the signs of possessing one was the most terrible of failures. But no matter how many times I explained to the priest that I really was not all that anxious to go to the seminary, the answer was always the same: all signs pointed to my having been called; I must test my Vocation to see whether it was genuine; and the only way to do that was to enter a seminary and see, once and for all, if I had not been privileged by the grace of God to spend my life as a priest.

As I grew, it grew with me; it grew stronger, if anything, rather than weaker. I remember thinking up schemes by which I might manage to be both a priest and a fighter pilot at the same time. Eventually, however, I recognized the truth; I could not say I liked it, but my Vocation was there, and there was only one thing I could do about it. I got a black suit, with my parents' help, and a steamer trunk at Boggs and Buhl's Department Store (difficult items to find in wartime). I got on a train, which was really a troop train, and went off to the preparatory seminary at Notre Dame, Indiana. By that August I had been prepared, and so I got on the truck with the others, to help save the world and to give my life to God in what was referred to by spiritual authorities as the Holocaust of Divine Love.

*　*　*

That was why I smiled at Billy Simmonds. At sixteen, he was ridiculously young; he had come to the seminary at the age of twelve, having gotten a dispensation from Rome to come so early. He was precociously bright, able to read Greek and Latin. He knew everything about the religious life and the Church and Canon Law and Breviaries and the Novitiate and the order and the priesthood, and he so instructed me. I had come in my third year of high school. We faced nine more years together if we stayed—one of Novitiate, four of Philosophy, and four more of Theology. He knew nothing about the war or what was going on in the world, and I instructed him. He had a beautiful high voice which led us in the Sacred Liturgy. His little black suit seemed the perfect uniform, and even the fact that he insisted on wearing cowboy boots with it did not destroy the impression. And yet I could sense as we drew nearer to the Novitiate that Billy, though he was happy, was frightened, too. That was the reason for his darting looks at me, and that was the reason for all his Judas Priests. In a way, we were very much the same.

On the back of the truck we sang. Billy led us, mostly in cowboy songs. We sang about the streets of Laredo and the wind blowing free and the Red River Valley and a lot about "little dogies" (Billy, though he was from Ohio, had always wanted to be a cowboy). Then, as the truck left South Bend, we sang about the Halls of Montezuma and the Field Artillery and trampling out the vineyards. We began calling one another "Mister," for that was how we would have to talk for the next twelve months. Mister Hanratty and Mister Skeffington argued theology on the floor of the truck, while Mister Kaminsky amused himself by being tail gunner out the back: each time a car passed he would gun it down as though it were a Jap Zero or a German Messerschmitt, shouting "Doo-*Doom!*" as though it had exploded; then he would mark down an invisible Rising Sun or Swastika on the railing of the truck. Finally, at the outskirts of the town of Rolling Prairie, in the middle of "Praise the Lord and Pass the Ammunition" we knew we were coming to the end of our journey and we stopped singing.

Suddenly Billy's hand touched my shoulder. "Listen, Mister!" he said. I listened, but didn't hear anything and asked him what we were listening for. "Can't you hear it?" he asked. "It's the big bell in the Novitiate tower. *Judas Priest!*" he said, shuddering with excitement. He explained to me that everything in the Novitiate was kept strictly under control of the sound of that bell. Whether you ate or drank or woke or slept, everything was done precisely to its sound. Bells were baptized like people, he said, and were actually given names. The huge one in the Novitiate tower was from Oberammergau in Bavaria, and was called "Augustine"—it could be heard twenty miles. I listened, but could hear nothing.

Brother Meinrad Kriegspieler slowed the truck down and turned into a long lane lined with barbed-wire fences, and we knew we were on the grounds of the Novitiate cattle farm, though the building itself was two miles farther. I strained with Billy to see what it was like. "There it is!" he said, and the huge structure rose up over us, dominating everything. The first things I noticed were the swallows flying endlessly in and out of the bell tower against the blue August sky. When I looked at the building itself, I thought it was beautiful, of course, but even darker and more severe than I had been prepared for.

In the last few moments in which we were allowed to speak, Billy told me as much as he could. We would be taken to our rooms or "cells," and later in the evening we would go to Chapel, where Father Master would instruct us on the topic of Vocation. But first, in the courtyard, Brother Meinrad would read off the list of jobs or "obediences" each one of us would have for the year. The most important was the job of Cantor, for he led everybody in the daily singing of the Divine Office. We both knew that Billy would have that. The next most important was the job of being Regulator, for whoever was given that spent all his time ringing the bell and looking at the clock. He had to get up in the morning to wake everybody at five o'clock, and it was very difficult. Nobody wanted it, for, to tell the truth, nobody really *liked* whoever was Regulator.

In the last seconds Billy turned and looked at me intensely. I knew he wanted to say something important to me and was wondering how far I might be trusted. Finally, he said, "We are friends—at least, you know me better than anyone else. Promise me. If I weaken, do not let me give in. I've got to make it. No matter what I do or say, don't listen to me. *Don't help me quit.* I will not be able to go on living if it is not as a priest." Then, with a sweeping gesture that took in, I thought, the vows, the priesthood, and a good deal of the prairie itself, he said, "This is the one thing I want."

He looked at me. I understood perfectly, and I nodded. "Same with me. Of course, I would want you to treat me exactly the same." We shook on it, swearing a kind of eternal allegiance to one another. We would be priests together.

"Now watch what happens," he said quickly as the

50

truck stopped. "Brother Kriegspieler is a little bit . . . strange. There's something wrong with him—that's why he's out here. He's always doing funny things, but it's meant in kindness, to help you get through the year. Make friends with him—you'll eat lots of extra desserts."

Brother Meinrad jumped from the cab, drawing himself up into an exaggerated attitude of "attention," pretending to be a German officer. I had heard about it; it was his one great joke, and he played it over and over: we were the Jews, you see, and Brother Meinrad was everything from Herr Kommandant to Der Führer himself. Sometimes, they said, he could be quite funny about it and made you laugh, because, after all, it was only a joke.

"*Choos!*" I heard him shout, in a ridiculous accent. "*Choos! Line up!*"

Rather sheepishly, for though it was a joke we were not sure how far it extended, we began getting off the truck. A piece of fencing that formed the tailgate of the truck was lowered to form a ladder, and as we got off we formed two rows. First, Brother Meinrad strode down the two lines passing out little strips of linen cloth with numbers on them. It turned out they were our laundry tags: each novice was given a number, to be sewn on everything we wore. I looked down at mine; 421, with a little plus sign in front of it, inside a small oval. For the rest of the Novitiate, for the rest of my religious life, I would be +421. It would be inside the collars of my shirts, and on my shorts and socks; and even when I took out my handkerchief to sneeze or blow my nose, the little circle would be there: you are +421, it would say. I stole a look at Billy's: his number was +30.

Brother Meinrad then took out a piece of paper and

began reading out the list of assignments or obediences for the year. Mister Zimmer was given the cow barn, and Mister Coon and Mister Reedy got the pig barn. Mister Dark got chickens. Finally, Mister Simmonds, as we all expected, was named Cantor, and a very great tension built up over the group: Brother Kriegspieler had saved the best for last.

It was then I noticed that he held a bell in his hands, a bronze bell that he had been concealing all the while behind his back. He pulled it out to let us see it and then, like a magician, concealed it once more. He started slowly down the rows; he was Herr Kommandant again, inspecting the troops. He savored the moment, stopping first at little Mister Sorin from New Orleans and frightening him that *he* might be the Regulator; then he went to Mister Jenkins, who had trouble to keep from laughing. When he came to Mister Kaminsky and paused, Mister Kaminsky pointed his finger at him and said, "Doo-*Doom!*" pretending to have a gun. Brother Meinrad scowled—that was breaking silence—and moved on, past Mister Simmonds. He stopped at me, smiled, and handed me the bell. I was Regulator.

A great roar of laughter went up. I was famous for being late; I never owned a watch and usually did not know what time it was. In the prep seminary I had been continually reprimanded by Father Grimm and Father Fiedler and warned that if I did not improve I would have to leave, that I would be dismissed, and that I could never be a priest, for a priest had to know what time it was.

I tried to smile back as I took the bell. Brother Meinrad beckoned me up to take his place in front of the men; I did so and waited to be told what to do next. He said something in German which I did not understand, but it contained the word *Arbeit* (work), which we all knew was his favorite word. *"Mach schnell,"* he said quietly, and indicated that I should ring the bell and lead the men into the interior of the Novitiate. I managed to give it a few clangs, and then I led my brothers into the dark old building. Over the door was carved the words CRUX SPES UNICA, the order's motto: "The Cross, Our Only Hope." After we passed under it, each man was led to his cell. The Novitiate had begun.

"You are a chosen people, a priesthood set apart!" said Father Master in his opening talk, later that evening. "This was rightly said of old," he continued, "to the Children of Israel, through their prophets. It is rightly said now, once again, even more rightly, to you, to every man taken from among men to be ordained in the things of God, for it is told you through the divine wisdom and authority of Holy Mother the Church and is therefore infallible.

"Sacred Scripture tells us. Some men there are who are eunuchs. Some men are eunuchs from their mother's womb. Some are made eunuchs by their fellow man. I would not have you ignorant," Father Master added by way of parenthesis, "I would have no person under my care ignorant; but in the corrupt days of the Middle Ages certain misguided people actually had operations performed—*i castrati* they are called in the Italian language— whereby their singing voices would be enhanced. This is of no concern to us, for we are in the twentieth century. And, finally, some men make themselves eunuchs for the Kingdom of Heaven's sake.

"It is the one thing that is necessary, my dear young

men, the *Unum Necessarium*. In that splendid passage wherein Vocation is described, where Our Lord quintessentially told the Rich Young Man—who was rich in the things of this world, who had many things to live for— what it meant to have a Vocation, He said to the young man who would be perfect, 'There is still one thing that is necessary: give up all things, and come, follow me.' And you know what happened. That young man—that *good* young man—it is said, in Sacred Scripture, that he turned away, *'for he had many possessions!'*

"The Apostles came to Jesus and said, That we must give up our freedom, and all things to follow you, it is a hard saying. And you know what Christ said? In the splendid Latin of the Vulgate it reads *'Qui potest capere, capeat!'* He who is able to take, let him take!"

These last words were delivered with a tremendous effect; you could hear them echoing down the main corridor after he said them. *"Qui potest capere, capeat!"* he said again. "To the world, this is foolishness. It is foolish to give up human love, ownership, and, most important of all, our freedom. *'Astiterunt Reges terrae,'* says the psalm that you will sing: See how the Gentiles devise vain things, and the nations unite against God's Anointed! Make no mistake; you are assuming a heavy burden. You have come here in response to the call of God; you come to answer nothing less than Christ's command, 'Be ye perfect, as your Heavenly Father is perfect.' You come to this Novitiate for nothing less than to seek perfection itself."

We had many aids to do this. The Rule of Silence, by which we did not speak; the Rule of Recollection, by which we shut out everything and did not think except to think about the one thing that was necessary; the Rule of Obedience, by which we desired nothing except the will of God manifested to us by the orders of the legitimate Superior. The movements of the body were taken care of by the Rule of Regular Discipline. ("If a man's trouble is below his belt," Father Master added in a sardonic tone, "he has no business, of course, being here; novices should be beyond that.")

Father Master now came to his main point of the evening. It was the matter of time, and promptness, and exactitude in the answering of the bell: this more than anything else would assure that we would have a successful Novitiate year and become candidates for Profession. *"A man must learn to tell time,"* said Father Master, almost shouting at us. "It is no exaggeration to say that the religious life consists essentially in being in the right place at the right time. It is the one thing in your life that you can be infallibly certain about. When you hear the sound of the bell, my young men, it is God Himself speaking to you, and the bell is rightly called *Vox Dei*, the Voice of God. When you answer it promptly and precisely, you know that you are being pleasing to God as no man is, for each of you is giving up his own free will and making of his life a holocaust. God is no longer God of the Jews, to be pleased by burnt offering. *That was the Old Testament.* No! He is your God now, and it is through the devout self-immolation of young people like yourselves that He chooses to be honored.

"Learn, therefore, my dear novices, what time it is. Set your watches by the great Oberammergau bell in the Chapel tower; it is never wrong. Be wise virgins, ready for the Bridegroom, for it is late, always much later than when you first heard the good tidings of Redemption: 'For ye know not the day nor the hour.' "

Father Master then went on to tell us something that was very interesting, something that I had never heard about before, nor, indeed, had dreamed existed. He explained to us that, so important in the Economy of Salvation was the element of time that the Church taught, not one, but *four* different ways of telling it. The hour of midnight, for example, was extremely important in the life of the Church, for so many grave obligations either began or terminated on the stroke of midnight. He quickly went through four types, and showed us the four ways of computing midnight.

The first kind of Time, Sidereal or Celestial, he said, did not concern us: it concerned only astronomers. The second, Standard Time, might seem to us to be True Time, but it was not, for it was of course arbitrarily divided up by man for his own use into time zones; to find True Time, you had in fact to add or subtract minutes and seconds, depending upon where in the time zone you were located. It was useless to us, too, during the Novitiate year, since Rolling Prairie was situated eleven minutes to the east of the center of its zone. For us to calculate True Midnight, for example, we would have to subtract eleven minutes from the clock, which would of course be useless, for when the clocks in Rolling Prairie showed eleven minutes to twelve, True Midnight had already occurred! He went on to tell us about True or Sun Time, and about special types, such as Daylight Saving, and, of course, what actually was being observed by the nation: War Time.

After he concluded the matter, he remarked that it all might seem irrelevant to us, but it was not. "My dear young men, a year is made up of weeks and months and days and hours. At the end of eight days, your initial Retreat, you will receive the Holy Habit of the Order. It will, fittingly enough, be the Feast of the Transfiguration of Christ; later on that same morning you will be witnesses to the First Profession of Vows by the members of this year's class. The seasons will then turn. Summer will become autumn, and autumn, winter; the Church's Liturgy will sing you through Advent, to Christmas, into the new year, and the year of Our Lord 1944 will become the year of Our Lord 1945. Lent will come, with its fast, and Holy Week, and you will die with Christ, only to rise with Him again on Easter morning. And at last, in God's time, if you are worthy, you will in that year of Our Lord 1945, on the Feast of the Transfiguration of Our Lord, August the sixth, you, too, will profess your vows, and in so doing make of your life a perfect holocaust for God."

Father Master concluded his talk with a warning. It would not be easy. There would be times during our Novitiate year when we would be tempted to give up, to seek permission to leave, to escape the heavy obligations of the religious life, to return to families and friends and to the world and its lesser concerns. There would be times when even the best of us would then feel that he was throwing away his young life for nothing; we would then feel that we were going through what the spiritual writers called the Dark Night of the Soul, and that God had abandoned us. "Make no mistake," he said sharply, "God will not abandon you, no more than He abandoned His Chosen People, for God never abandons those who place their trust in Him.

"Begin, then, tonight," he concluded. "When the bell

has sounded, initiating this first of all the nightly Grand Silences of your Novitiate, beg, pray, beseech Almighty God that all these things may come to pass."

After he had finished, Father Master rose, went to the center of the sanctuary, genuflected solemnly before the Tabernacle, and returned to his pew in the back of the Chapel. Mister Simmonds put away a notebook (in which he had fiercely been writing down what Father Master had said, for later study), came to his feet, and led us in the singing of Vespers: "Blessed is the Lord Our God," he sang, "for He has visited us and come at last to save His People, Israel." Finally, Compline, the Night Prayer of the Church, was sung, and Billy sang to God for us about the swift-departing light, asking for peace in sleep, and ending with Christ's last prayer on the cross: "Father, into Thy hands I commend my spirit."

When the last words of the beautiful Gregorian plainchant were sung, I picked up my bell and rang it one clang, as I had been carefully instructed to. With that began the Grand Silence, which was to last all night.

Before going up to my cell, in a final meditation in the Chapel, I prayed as I had been told to: I begged and beseeched Almighty God that it would happen—that I would have a successful Novitiate, that I would prove equal to the task of making my life a holocaust for God, and that, a year to the day, I would be found worthy to pronounce my vows.

In my cell, however, after I had, in effect, put everyone else to bed, I found that I could not sleep. In reality, I was afraid to sleep for fear I would not wake in the morning to get everyone else up at five o'clock. Besides, it had been a hectic day, a day in which there had been no time to think. I tried to fall asleep—even in private, alone where only God could see me, I knew that I was under the obligation to sleep, and so I tried. I was unsuccessful; songs kept coming back into my head, especially one from the back of the truck, that Billy had sung, a cowboy song about a calf being led to market:

> Calves are easily bound and slaughtered,
> Never knowing the reason why,
> But whoever treasures freedom
> Like the swallow has learned to fly.

It went on about the winds blowing free in the chorus, and as I lay awake trying to sleep, the thin little voice of Billy kept coming back to me, keeping me awake.

I came to a rather startling thought: I did not like the Novitiate. I hesitated to admit it, but eventually, in the night, I had to. I more than did not like it, I feared it; and, in a way, I detested it. I wished I could run away to the war and become a carrier pilot, or maybe join the Marines and fight in places like the island of Saipan or Guadalcanal. Unfortunately, however, there was little I could do about it. I had to test my Vocation and this was the only way to do it. At least I was certain of one thing: I would do it well, even though I disliked it. I would seek perfection, as God and the Church demanded. With a twinge of guilt I recalled that I had not taken notes as Billy had; I was not even off to a good beginning. I would get a notebook at once; I would take down everything that was told me; I would meditate on those thoughts, and use them to learn the Practice of the Presence of God. And in the end, with God's grace, I would become perfect and pleasing to Him.

I turned over and went to sleep. The alarm sounded

and I thought I had made a mistake setting it, for it was still dark; but the clock was right—the time was 4:45 A.M. I jumped into my robe, with its +421 already sewn neatly into its collar, and went down into the cold main corridor and waited for Augustine in the tower to sound. For a moment I was afraid to ring the bell. The huge place seemed so silent and so dark I wondered if I might not be dreaming, that I might not really be supposed to wake anybody. But Augustine sounded, and I thought of the will of God; I swallowed hard, took a deep breath, and started to ring my smaller bell. At first it made a ridiculous sound—the clapper slithered around the side, not making a true ring; but I began to catch on to it, and by the time I reached the Professed Corridor it sounded right. I stopped and shouted out as loud as I could, *"Benedicamus Domino!"* and here and there, in sleepy voices, I heard the words *"Deo Gratias,"* my brothers in Christ thanking God for being awakened. I went on to wake the rest of the house, and was relieved that I had, at least, begun correctly.

I became a good bell-ringer after that. I became a fine, rigorous person, indeed, conscious of the clock, and on time, always. I rang my brothers to everything—to prayer and meals and choir and recreation. But most of all it was to the barns I rang them—to the pig barn and to the horse barn and to the dairy barn, and of course to the greatest barn of all, the slaughterhouse itself, for the Novitiate farm, more than anything else, consisted in that kind of operation. I knew that it did not make me popular—that as soon as people saw me coming they thought of unpleasant things. Only Mister Simmonds seemed not to mind. He had warned me; but I reasoned that it was my sacred obedience, that it was the will of God, and that it was my special test in the Novitiate.

At the end of the Retreat, on the Feast of Transfiguration of Our Lord, on August 6, I was invested in the holy habit, and my entire class became true novices. Later in the morning I was appointed to stand at Father Master's side during the vow ceremonies for the departing class, and tie up the cinctures for the new *professori*.

"Gloria et honore coronasti eum!" intoned Mister Simmonds from the choir loft; but I had the more solemn duty: as each man came up the aisle carrying his Vow Formula and knelt down before the huge old Missal Book in Father Master's lap to freely promise his life in dedication to the highest good of all, I stood ready at hand, first with a pen for him to sign with, and then to help tie the cincture around the waist as each one finished, for the knot was difficult to make. They all had trouble pronouncing the words for the year 1944 in Latin: *Millesimo, nongentesimo, quadragesimo quarto.* And each time, after each one had given out his *quadragesimo quarto*, I held out to him and helped fasten around his waist the heavy, silken, almost velvet cord. And as I did so I found myself devoutly wishing that I could be in his place, that it would already be next year, with some other new young novice doing exactly the same for me.

The departure on the truck of the newly professed to study Dogmatic Theology, the next stage of training for the priesthood, left the Novitiate empty and lonely, for we had made friends with them. We had lapses, too, in keeping some of the rules. At first, when the Novitiate was still new, we amused ourselves. For a while, during recreation in the hour after supper, when we were allowed to speak, we went through a spell of calling one another by number instead of names. "Mister 421!" I would hear Mister Kaminsky call out. "Mister 421!" "Yes, Mister 83, what is it?" I would answer, and so on. We asked Billy what his number was, and he announced solemnly, "Thirty," and we all laughed—it seemed so short, and such a good number for him.

But later that evening word came down from Father Master's office that we were breaking the Rule of Address, that we were to stop referring to one another as numbers.

And very early we were loaned out as a group to a nearby orchard farmer at Williams Orchards. He had a full crop of peaches and, his own sons gone off to war, had no one to harvest them. He was our neighbor, and so we helped him. All twenty of us were sent over, on the back of the truck again, and were shown the proper way to pick peaches. You were to fill up your fruit bucket, carefully; you were to walk over to the bushel basket, and then gently—very, very gently—so as not to damage the tender fruit—you were to release the little ropes that held the canvas bottom of the bucket, allowing the peaches to roll, *undamaged*, into the bushel basket.

Billy and I (or, that is, Mister Simmonds and I, of course) got ourselves assigned to the same row of trees. It was beautiful summery weather. Hour after hour we would climb the ladder up into the laden peach trees, looking out over the countryside and up into the clear air, and then descend to carefully deposit our burden in the baskets on the ground. We worked hard, for the glory of God and for our neighbor; we kept the Rule of Silence and the Rule of Recollection, so that we should be able to pray while we worked and, most of all, above all, practice the Presence of God.

That afternoon I had been especially successful in retaining custody of the eyes and ears, refusing to pay heed to distractions, concentrating on the peaches, and practicing the Presence of God by frequent aspirations such as "My Jesus, mercy!" and "Lord have mercy on us!" and many others. I found myself at the very top of a tree, looking up into the sky, when I noticed something that, with all due respect for the Rule of Recollection, I had scarcely been able to ignore the previous few days. It was an airplane, high up in the sky, flying westward. I knew a lot about planes: this was a bomber, and it was a new kind. It was, I knew, not just an old Flying Fortress—those I had seen all through my childhood. This I recognized as something new, and much larger, with a tremendous deadly snout on it and a high, high tail. The planes flew very high, and always westward as they passed over the Novitiate: they were obviously headed for the Pacific Theater. What were they? I wondered. What gigantic new weapon had my country created? I descended and walked over, past Mister Simmonds, to the bushel basket.

I stood there looking downward for a moment. Then, *"Bombs away!"* I shouted, breaking silence, and letting the peaches fall violently and bruisingly into the bushel basket below.

Mister Coon in the next row overheard me and laughed delightedly. Mister Simmonds looked at me, startled. He may have wanted to say "Judas Priest!" a few times, but if he did, he controlled the urge. Instead he walked calmly over to the receptacle and poured his own peaches, gently and properly, into it. I felt corrected. He really was perfect, impossibly so; already he had transformed himself into such a perfect novice that no Rule could ask more from a human being.

All the same, I was not the worst. There was one novice, Mister Eddie O'Donnell, who lived totally in his imagination. For him the war was omnipresent and he made it so to everyone around him. He sounded like a war movie, for his talk was full of "Krauts" and "Heinies." Instead of working, he spent whole work periods sneaking up on "Japs" through the bean rows and the strawberry patches, and turned his part of the farm into Guadalcanal or Normandy. His favorite trick was to shout (in the solemn silence), "Hand grenade! Fall on it!" Then he would dive to the ground, clutching it to his breast, to save the rest of us—his buddies. His last words were always "The Krauts got me!"

One September afternoon as he pulled his routine, Brother Meinrad stepped out of the bushes and said, "Mister O'Donnell, come with me," and took him up to Father Master's office. Eddie left four days later, to join the Marines.

Our mood changed as we became more aware of the heavy reality of the Novitiate year. On the weekly Community Walk on Sunday afternoon, the only time we were allowed out, off the grounds, some people like Mister Conroy or Mister Knous still managed a frolicsome attitude for a while, at least until we got down to the stockyards of La Porte, where we would have to turn around to come back. But that stopped, too, and the bleak and wintry dark late afternoons, along endless cornfields and sow pens, with the barbed-wire fences that stretched to the horizon and beyond that to infinity, made each of us think over and over about such things as why he was there and how long he would last.

There were occasional diversions, but very few. I discovered that Brother Meinrad had another side to him. When he came in from work and went to his room, I would hear his phonograph playing music endlessly. It was all German music, usually Bach or Wagner or Beethoven. His favorite was Beethoven's Ninth, the Choral Symphony, and when he played that, Brother would lift his voice and join in the splendid German, and the Professed Corridor would be filled with *"Gotterfunken's"* and *"Feuertrunken's"* and *"Alle Menschen's."* Whenever that happened, or whenever I heard the great opening four notes of the Fifth—the "dot-dot-dot-dash" of Churchill's "V for Victory" speech—I would run and get Billy, and, without breaking the Rule of Silence, or at least breaking it only as little as was necessary, we would together go up to listen outside Brother's door. "What's he singing?" I would ask, and Billy would explain the German of Schiller's "Ode to Joy": how *"Freude"* was Joy—the Daughter of Elysium—and that all men became brothers under her starry wings. We kept ourselves ready to walk off in different directions as though nothing were happening, if anyone came. But when we were very brave and no one interrupted us, as the words came up to *"Gepruft im Tod"* we found ourselves singing, to the music coming through the door, about how there must be something—*something*—faithful unto death; how there must be something—One—above the starry heavens of the night, that would last forever and remain faithful to the end. It moved me deeply, and for the rest of the Novitiate, and, indeed, for the

rest of my life, I came to hear myself, while I was working, shouting meaninglessly words like *"Bruder!"* or
"Welt!," only in my mind, where no one could hear me.

Then one day, when I was standing outside the door
alone, not having been able to find Mister Simmonds,
Brother opened the door suddenly and found me. He
looked at me, surprised, and was about to berate me.
But then he only nodded, and we both walked away.

It became very hard. As Regulator, because I had to
keep close to the bell, I had to remain in the house in
the afternoons while everyone else went out to work. I
was assigned, like all Regulators, to sweeping the Basement Chapel. This was a complex of basement corridors
and side altars hidden away in the subterranean darkness beneath the Main Chapel. It was referred to as "the
Polish Corridor" because in the past so many novices
with Polish names had been assigned there. It was a
place to which few people ever came, for it was dark and
totally without daylight. Yet, for some reason I could not
figure out, it required sweeping every day—careful,
methodical sweeping with a big broom and buckets of
dampened sawdust. It was not really enough work to
occupy the whole two and a half hours of work period,
and time became very tedious. I mentioned this to Father
Master during Spiritual Directions, but he only smiled
and pointed out that it offered unparalleled opportunity
for Meditation, and that a man was very close to God
down there.

I had just turned eighteen. And as I walked out of
Father Master's office I reflected that, whatever other
young men of my age were doing, it was clear that I was
going to spend the eighteenth year of my life down in
that place, with the faded aroma of church linens and of

incense and, of course, the eternal smell of dampened sawdust on the floor.

And so the life of the farm, with all its interesting activity, was kept far from me. I thought often of the happy day out in the peach orchard with Billy, but as fall came that memory faded. I struggled manfully to practice the Presence of God; I knew that obedience—the one thing that was necessary—was all that mattered; I was in the Novitiate, after all, to perfect myself. Yet it was awful; and it was very difficult sometimes, down there in the darkness, in spite of all I had been told, to keep from wondering if I was not a young man entering into some form of the Dark Night of the Soul.

I lost track of Billy ("Old Mister Thirty," he now called himself); indeed, it might almost be said that I lost track of my fellow man. I only heard him; he became a voice singing out the Church's Liturgy: all those prayers, promises, arguments, failures, shouts, cries for help, hymns of victory, of comfort and affliction, which together tell the story of man's endless search for a redeemer, for someone to come and save him. *"O Adonai!"* he would cry out, or *"O Oriens!"* in the Great Antiphons of Advent, or *"Pange Lingua"* during Holy Hours, or *"Vindica Sanguinem!"* during Solemn High Mass. His voice, though it was beautiful, seemed increasingly sad and distant, although I wondered if it was not my imagination—if *I* was the one going through something, while he was all right.

One morning in Conference, however, something happened which, for the first time, gave me reason to think that my friend's condition might well be worse than my own.

Father Master had been giving us our first conference

on ownership, as preparation for the Vow of Poverty. He had explained how we really were not capable of possessing anything once we had made our vows—that we were *incapax*, as he called it—that we had given up ownership entirely, and that the *ad usum* mark we were to put above our name on books and on anything else we were tempted to call our own meant simply "for the use of," not "for the possession of." It was good training for the kind of life we would lead; we were to think little of the things of this world and place our whole concern on that other world yet to come.

After he had finished the rather technical lecture detailing all the possible ways of owning, Father Master asked, as he always did, whether anybody had any questions. Very rarely did anybody take him up on this; it was generally acknowledged that Father Master really did not see why there should be many questions after his very thorough way of explaining things, and the few times a novice did gain the courage, in the heavy silence which followed the talks, to ask how or why a certain thing should be so, we all watched for Father Master's famous temper to manifest itself.

That morning, however, after the Poverty lecture, there was a little stir behind me and to the left; I was afraid to turn my head to look, but I had found out that by staring intensely off into the distance in front of me I could often in a way see what was going on around me without appearing to. That morning by looking very hard I was able to see one small part of the mass of black behind me detach itself a little from the rest. Mister Simmonds had stood up; he had no doubt been writing notes intently on what had been said, and now he wanted to clarify something.

"Yes, Mister?" Father Master said.

"Father Master," said Billy in a thoughtful voice, "I have a question about Poverty, but first I would like to ask about Time. We sing Matins, the Morning Song of the Church, at five o'clock in the evening, then we sing Little Hours—which should be in the afternoon—in the morning, and that leaves Vespers and Compline, the Night Prayer of the Church, to be done at one-thirty. It seems off; all the words about being asleep are during the day, and the ones about being awake are at night!"

Father Master enjoyed the way the question was put. "The reason for that, Mister," he replied, smiling, "is simply the importance of midnight. So grave is the obligation to complete the office of the day that we anticipate, we say it ahead of time, so that we are never caught by the hour of midnight, which would be unthinkable. What is your other question?"

Billy sounded even more thoughtful this time. "I was just wondering, Father—you have explained ownership in all its ramifications, but I was wondering—who owns our bodies? Who do *we* belong to?"

He should not have asked it; I knew that at once. There was something wrong with that kind of question in the particular context, though I could not say just what. I shuddered a bit, though I would not be able to say why.

The question struck Father Master in a certain way, too; he began to get angry; I could see his skin starting to get red around his Roman collar, and his face strained with the effort to hold his temper. The fact that it was such a good Novice as Mister Simmonds who had asked the question did not help. Finally, he could not control it any more and he burst out in the voice we all knew he used when he had lost his temper, almost screaming: *"God* owns your bodies! Mister, *you belong to God!"* And with that he gathered his books and strode out of the room as though we were all impossibly stupid, the best of us little less dumb than the very beasts of the field.

After that Billy asked no more questions, nor, for a very long time, did anyone else; anyone who had any questions tended very much to keep them to himself. I worried about Mister Simmonds after that; he seemed to be going off on a direction by himself that might bring harm; but, of course, it would be his misfortune—I had my own problems.

Lost in the darkness of the Basement Chapel, I played games so that Time, dreadful, empty, silent Time, would pass on—so that the awful, terrible year of 1944 would move on, would hurry on, and become glorious, joyful 1945, so that the month of August 1945 would finally come with all it signified: that my time of trial would be over, and that I would win my fight with myself.

To help Time along, however, I played games. One dark afternoon that was proving especially dreary, when I seemed to be moving the sawdust around to no particular purpose, and the basement corridor seemed awfully far removed from the Presence of God, so that I was even beginning to really doubt that it could be pleasing to Him to have me down there sweeping something that obviously did not need sweeping, I noticed something: the three brass drain covers in the floor. It was not the first time I noticed them—they were the only bright things in the basement and I had swept around and over them every dreadful work period from the beginning of my Novitiate; no, what I noticed was their particular positioning: a person with any kind of eye for such things could easily see that the entire layout of the floor strongly resembled the map of Europe, if you thought of the three drain covers as the cities of Rome, Paris, and Berlin. I stopped to consider what Rule I could possibly be breaking if, instead of sweeping the floor in the usual boring, straightforward manner, I actually made it all mean something. I decided that by turning the piles of sawdust into moving armies I could parallel exactly what was going on at that moment in Europe, one bronze circle representing Rome, one for Paris, and one for Berlin.

I did so. Each day after that I assembled the armies so as to represent the Allies coming from one direction past Paris, and General Mark Clark's Eighth Army going up the center past Rome, and the Russians coming from the other side to close in on Berlin. The game varied as each day I changed the scenario. From my meager, and mostly illicit, sources of information about what was going on in the world, I knew that Eisenhower and Patton had already freed Paris, and that Rome had been taken, too (we had prayed in Chapel for the safety of the Holy Father); the real excitement was who would take Berlin? Some days I let the Russians get awfully close, but in the end, of course, the Americans always ended up the victors. When that happened I had to move awfully fast—if Father Master, *or anyone*, noticed the huge pile of sawdust in front of the altar rail, he would certainly wonder what was going on.

One afternoon, in fact, I thought I heard someone in the sacristy. Nothing happened, but a week later, just as I was closing in on Berlin with the Russians, Brother Meinrad strode out into the Chapel and asked me what was I doing, playing? Being a novice, I had to respond with the truth when asked; I was humiliated, but told him that the brass cover represented Berlin. He snarled in delighted laughter, but when he saw that the Russians were winning, Brother Meinrad ripped the broom out of my hands and pushed that pile of sawdust back where it came from. *"Heraus mit dir!"* he shouted, Away with you! Then he turned to me.

"You are much too old a fellow to be playing games," he said with a smile, handing me back my broom. "Tomorrow report to the barns, and I will give you a man's work!" With that he stepped down the center aisle over the sawdust and out of the Chapel.

I had heard that the Novitiate farm was really a complete cattle-slaughtering operation, and that the Professed Brothers had all the equipment of a great meat-packing plant. But I was not prepared for what I saw the first time I walked into the great slaughterhouse. The first things I saw were men standing ankle deep in blood. Other men were sharpening knives. Huge clamps were being used to rip off the hides of steers. One man, presumably a Brother, was standing in the midst of a mass of intestines while he slitted each animal from gut to groin. I heard the insistent, grating whine of a buzz saw someplace, and looked over: it was slicing off hooves.

I had been prepared for blood, but not that much. Every worker was covered with it. There were endless instruments of torment, too: knives, axes, saws, forceps, grindstones, cleavers, pliers, hammers, and drills. But, most of all, there were hooks. A conveyor belt endlessly full of them passed right by me: it came up to my face and then passed above me, hook after hook, each one bearing the head of a lamb, which looked at me, wide-eyed in death. And of course there were the great hoses, to wash away the blood.

I wanted to get back outside, for I was afraid I would be sick. A man came up to me, laughing; he, too, was covered with blood, at least his rubbery uniform was. He was being friendly: "Your first time," he said. "You'll get used to it." He made a movement as if to put his rubber-covered arm around my shoulders and I remembered the blood, so I made a ducking movement. He laughed; it was Brother Meinrad. I managed not to throw up. "You'll be a smart old buck yet," he said. "You'll get used to it."

You did have to get used to it; we all knew that you had to become a man. That was what the Novitiate was all about. And yet it took me a long time, and some things I never did get used to.

The slaughter of a calf, for instance. Brother took care of each one of those himself. They never seemed to sense the presence of death. Each calf invariably allowed itself to be led into the slaughter pen by what was called the Judas Goat, which then of course departed safely. The calf would be left looking straight at Brother Meinrad, who was always strained and nervous. I could see his knuckles white on the shaft of the sledgehammer. I had not known exactly how it was done. The calf's meditative head was held; Meinrad's whole form tensed with anticipation of what he was about to do. Then he hit the forehead of the animal, and the calf went down with its two forelegs splayed out ridiculously, as though the whole thing were an animated cartoon. At once Meinrad leaped from the hammer to the knife and quickly—

mercifully, perhaps, as he would claim—slit the animal's throat to let the blood out. We novices, cumbersomely, and pretending that it did not bother us, hooked the carcass up by the heels and hung it on a meat hook. Then we got ready for the next calf.

I was learning, I suppose. But it never seemed to get any better. Always there was some new surprise, some harshness I had not known about. One time Brother sent me to the pig barn with four other novices. When I found out what we had to do, I was quite frightened: Brother wanted to do something to Chester, the huge boar. He needed us to hold Chester in his sty. Five of us leaned against the boar and held him against the side of his pen. Chester had been breaking out of it, escaping by lifting up the fence with his powerful snout, and now Brother was going to put metal clips into his nose to discourage him from rooting. While we had the huge boar immobilized ("Watch your feet," someone said, "he can bite right through a boot"), Meinrad planted the clips, to the agonized shrieks of Chester. Then, grinning, Brother seized the opportunity to do something else he had wanted to do for a long time: to break back the huge saber teeth. It was awful; he took a large pliers and simply broke poor Chester's great eyeteeth out of the corners of his mouth. Then he let him go, and I saw Chester feeling the empty places with his tongue, like a child after the dentist. I was glad to be through with it.

But I was not through with it. Brother Meinrad was making good his word. Next day they needed novices to hold the four legs of each of the males of the sow's new litter: they were to have an operation performed on them so that they would produce more meat. I hated it, for through each little animal's legs I could feel his terror and pain so that it almost turned my stomach. During the surgery itself the little pigs were too frightened to squeal, but when Brother applied a bluish antiseptic, it cauterized the cut, and they screamed all afternoon and on into the evening, so that other novices could hear it all through the whole Novitiate. And Mister Simmonds, who had replaced me at my endless task of sweeping the basement, said at the supper table where we were given a *Deo Gratias* and allowed to speak, "I could hear it all the way down in the Basement Chapel. What were you doing to them?"

The whole table looked at me; some already knew, of course, but others around the table looked at me with blank, ignorant stares. I became a bit embarrassed, picked up the bread dish, and almost did not say anything; instead, I turned my lips into a smile and looked away, as though I were a seasoned cowhand. "We were de-balling them, Mister Simmonds," I said, and laughed, the way I had seen Meinrad laugh all afternoon.

Poor Billy. He had come to the Novitiate thinking he was a cowboy, singing all those songs about coyotes and dogies and buckoes and broncos, all that "a-walkin' " and "a-ridin.' " In the end he had been sent inside, to sweep the floor and do his choir practice. I smiled; he was no more a cowboy than I was a fighter pilot.

And he was in trouble.

One day after a hard afternoon's work, just before I was to go up and ring the bell, Brother Meinrad motioned me over to a little cubbyhole of an office off the side of the barn. He had a coffee pot there and some doughnuts. Incredibly, he offered me one and a cup of coffee.

I suppose we novices that year were very immature young men in our love of food, but things like ice cream or Coke or pie were terribly high in our scheme of things. When Brother Meinrad asked me to come in, sit down with him, and have a doughnut, it was the most delicious thing that could have happened. I felt very respectful.

"Would you like to hear about the war, Mister?" he asked. I nodded; it had been six months since I had heard anything from the world. "It is very bad," he said, shaking his head. "It's all over on the Eastern Front. This country should stop fighting Hitler and help him against the Russians. He never was our enemy anyway."

I nodded absently. I had really not heard properly what he said, so engrossed was I munching on the doughnut. Anyway, I had heard it all before. Everyone in the Novitiate knew that Meinrad believed the war to be an unjust one. Over and over he told everybody that the Treaty of Versailles had created it—the International Bankers and the Jews had placed Germany in an intolerable position. They had *created* Hitler themselves. And as far as the many things the newspapers said that he did wrong, why that was pure propaganda, ordered by Mister Roosevelt. "And they say Goebbels is a propagandist!" Brother shouted. "Why, compared to the *New York Times*, he is a *Kinderling!* I am tired of it!"

"Where is the front now?" I asked eagerly; I thirsted for this kind of information. "Where is General Patton?"

"They've taken Rome and Paris, as you probably know." I wondered if he thought back to my brass drains on the floor, among the sawdust. "Patton? He is almost to the Rhine. If something isn't done, he will be in Germany."

The coffee was finished, and the doughnut gone. I

looked at my watch and felt strangely uncomfortable. I got up, fearful of overdoing my stay. But as I did so, Brother Meinrad motioned me to remain where I was. I sat down again.

"Tell me, Mister," Brother asked, "how is your friend doing? Is he all right?"

I looked at him with some fear. "My friend? Which novice do you mean?" I asked.

Brother Meinrad smiled. *"Der Vogelsinger. Kikey.* Mister Simmonds, the Ohio cowboy."

"Mister Simmonds? He's doing all right, isn't he? He keeps the Rule perfectly."

Meinrad looked directly into my eyes, smiling a very knowledgeable smile. "Mister, take my advice: keep away from him. He is in trouble. He is full of questions, and he *worries* too much. *Keep away from anybody you see like that!"* He hissed this out quietly, intensely. That was what the coffee and doughnut had been for; Brother Meinrad was warning me of something; he was telling me to become wiser in some way, as if he was almost telling me that Billy's way would not work, that that way could only lead to disaster.

"And now, *heraus mit dir!"* he said, making a shoveling, scooping gesture, the way we did when shooing some farm animal up the chute, and he added, laughing, "You better get out of here or the other novices will start to call you the Judas Goat. *Der Judas-Zeigen!"*

When I came out, Mister Jenkins, whose chief fault was his inability to control his laughter, was standing inside the harness shop in a state of recollection, doubtless trying to practice the Presence of God while he waited for the end of work period. He was in a position, however, to hear perfectly the last words Brother had uttered. *"Der Judas-Zeigen . . ."* he started to giggle. *"Der Judas-Zeigen!"* he said, between gasps for breath. He laughed and laughed, leaning back against the wall, trying to control himself.

So that was it? I was embarrassed, first by Meinrad's comment and then by the unending ridicule of the laughter of Mister Jenkins, which followed me outside, and my skin felt that it was burning. Then my feeling changed to anger. Before starting up the hill to the Novitiate building, I deliberately and purposefully strode over to look at the Judas Goat in his pen. He was staring, glassy-eyed, on some distant prospect; he looked peculiarly absent-minded, for he was chewing, ruminating on some fodder. The bell around his neck made a soft tinkle when he moved, and he looked for all the world as though he were trying to think of something, something which eluded him, something that was ever on the verge of his memory but which, no matter how long he thought, he could not quite recall.

He looked so foolish and so human that I forgot my annoyance. I looked around, and since there was no one to hear but me, I said something. "You bloody fucking bastard, you!" I said to him. It made me feel better getting the words out; I had not talked that way in six months, and I laughed quietly as I walked off because there wasn't any Rule against talking to goats. I mounted the hill and rang the bell on time to end the work period. Then I headed for the showers.

And so, somehow, Christmas was coming on. As a result of my relationship with Meinrad, which I was careful to preserve without overdoing it in any way, I remained among those novices privileged to see nature in all its aspects. I saw the year go round in seasons. First, the hay creaking into the barns in late summer, and the spiders in their parachutes flying from tree to tree in September. I awoke one day to the swallows gone from their tower, where old Augustine still called out that it was late, late, much later than when first we had seen them, swooping in and out around him, from the back of the truck. I saw the stalks of corn shredded and sent into the silo as fodder, and we novices also sent to tramp it down with our feet, round and round in circles. And in the enforced silence of work I heard my mind bring up snatches from the Psalms and the Divine Office (the only language, increasingly, that ears heard and memory stored): "Thou shalt not muzzle the ox that threshes the grain," my feet would say as I tramped, or *"Venite Filii audite me"*—"Come my sons and listen unto me"—or *"Jam sol recedit igneus"*—"Now fades the light of the setting sun." I saw the leaves turn first and then fall, and so I rang myself and the men from summer to autumn into winter.

When the first, almost liturgical, snows fell, the *O Antiphons* were sung. Billy's voice lifted in the great cries of mankind waiting for a Savior: *"O Adonai!"* he sang, or "O Scepter of Israel and Key to the House of David!" or *"O Oriens!"*—Bright Star of Day. And we responded, to a man, praying ardently that God would come and dwell among men, and take us all from the torment of here below.

I wondered, of course, how Billy was doing; his chant was perfect and impersonal; and yet when he shouted man's cries to Heaven for help, I could not keep from feeling that it was from the depths of his own heart that he was shouting.

Things were not all that bad with me. As Christmas approached, I felt satisfied; I had survived. I had rung my brothers, rung them all, with very few mistakes, almost to the midpoint of the Novitiate year. I was proud, justifiably; in a way it was consoling to be Regulator, for during the long hours I had spent in the basement corridor I had had time to think. I came to the conclusion that if it was true that the sound of the bell was the Voice of God and that you knew infallibly when you obeyed its sound that you were being pleasing to God by being in the right place at the right time, why, then it followed that the person who rang it, the Regulator himself, was, in the very act of ringing it, and obeying, also certain that he, too, was being pleasing to God. It was good to be infallible about *something*; I was amazed at how far I had come.

On Christmas Eve everyone had to retire early, so as to be up for Midnight Mass. Only, instead of waking to the bell, the house was gently aroused by some of us in choir singing Christmas carols—*"Adeste Fideles"* and of course "Silent Night." The most touching moment came when we went up to old Father Mathias Oswald's room and softly sang outside his door (something we had prepared at length for) "Silent Night" in German: *"Stille Nacht! Heilige Nacht!"* so that he would awaken to the sounds that he had known as a boy, back in Bavaria, eighty years before.

At Midnight Mass, Father Master was clad in seemingly solid gold vestments. The *Consolamini* was sung: "Be consoled, O my people, be consoled, for behold, I am come, and am with you!"

And after reading the simple Gospel of the birth of Christ ("In the dark eternal night, O Lord, the night in the midst of its course, Thy Word came down to us, and the earth blossomed forth a Savior"), Father Master in his sermon announced to all the world the good news that salvation had come: "Tonight, in this winter of the Year of Our Lord 1944—a blessed year in which the life of the Supreme Pontiff has been spared and the sacred character of the City of Rome respected—much good has been accomplished. Men have reason to know that God has kept His Word, God has again kept His Promise, and once again His Chosen People are comforted by His Coming. Make no mistake: *He is among us! He has not delayed!*

"And you, my dear young novices, is there a man among you that does not have reason to look forward with confidence to the Year of Our Lord 1945? No man can tell ahead of time what that year will bring to the world, but you among all men have reason to find yourselves blessed in it: you are here hidden away with Christ—and Christ is God's! Do not be concerned with the world, for you have given up the world. Complete your part of the bargain: God has kept His. Look forward in 1945 to the perfection of your life, so that in the Holocaust of Divine Love you may seal it, on that bright day in August, with the victory that awaits you, the profession of your Vows of Poverty, Chastity, and Obedience."

For that brief while, on Christmas Eve of 1944, I could honestly say that I felt happy. As I clanged the bell and led the rest of the men out of their pews, I looked at my friend Mister Simmonds to see if he was happy. I looked at his face; he was tired and indescribably weary from it all, perhaps from all that singing. He seemed almost not to notice anything that was going on, and seemed driven along by some private misfortune that I knew nothing about. I wondered, to be honest, if he knew what time of year it was, or if he really cared.

And so the new year came.

One night late in January, long after Augustine had tolled eleven, I was startled by a knock at my cell door. My first thought was that it would be Brother Meinrad telling me about what kind of work I would do in the barns the next day, or Father Master making a change in schedule. I quickly jumped into my robe, pulled the belt tight around me, and opened the door. It was my neighbor from across the hall; it was Mister Simmonds.

No novice was ever to visit the room of another novice, day or night, under any circumstances whatever; that was the strictest rule in the Novitiate. To break that rule and be discovered meant that you would be dismissed at once and lose everything that you had come for—the vows, life in a religious order, even the priesthood itself. To me that was unthinkable.

I stood there looking at him. I stepped back, and more or less led him into my room. I did not know what to do, but I certainly did not want to keep my door open at that hour of the night.

"I have to talk to someone," he said. "You are my friend. I think I am going mad."

I had never heard anyone talk that way before.

"Father Master called me in today. He said that I had problems. I exhibited such anxiety over fundamental matters that it did not bode well for the future. He said he had been observing me, that I had a look on my face during lectures that made him feel I was not accepting things. Then he asked me what was I having difficulty with.

"I told him. I said that it was the Problem of Evil. That so many cruel things happened, on the farm, in the Novitiate, and in the world itself, that I had trouble believing in an Infinitely Good God. I said that I was praying over it, and that I was reading in the library to help me solve it.

"He hit the ceiling. 'The *Library!*' he shouted. 'The *library?* Mister, you are not competent to solve such problems! You have not even had Philosophy yet, and you are far away from Sacred Theology. You are not trained to deal with such things as the Problem of Evil.' "

Mister Simmonds was silent for a moment, and I became aware that I had not yet said anything; I decided to speak. "What did he tell you that you *should* do?" I asked, as a kind of politeness, under the circumstances.

"He told me that I should stop 'rooting and delving' among the 'tomes in the library.' He said that on the contrary my duty was to flee, to flee such thoughts when they occurred. And he said to me, 'Pray to God to resist such temptations. Should you not, should you on the contrary continue to entertain them, I shall have no other recourse than to consult the House Council, and to have you sent home.'

"He told me that to continue in this way would be a sin against the Light, that it was the sin against the Holy Spirit. . . ."

Billy stopped and looked at me. "I can't even sleep. You are my friend. What is your opinion? What do you say?"

I let him be, in silence. I was agitated myself, and really did not know what I was supposed to do. *Here is your fellow man,* I remember saying to myself; *treat him as you would be treated.* I wondered how that was. I tried desperately to remember all that Father Master had taught us, all that I had read and taken notes on from the beginning of the Novitiate year. Here is your first Soul, I heard myself saying. He is the first of all those who will ever come to you for aid. May God help you to say the right thing.

And so I told him, simply and honestly, what I hoped that anyone would tell me in such a situation: that, having consulted competent spiritual authority, having talked things over with his Director, and having been reassured that his soul still possessed the marks of a genuine Vocation, he should calm himself; that he was sure in fact he was still one of the People of God, one of God's own elect; that actually, indeed, he could now consider himself all but infallibly certain that he would be pleasing to God by remaining a novice and continuing the fight. Furthermore, that he could be sure that God would not abandon him, for God never abandoned anyone, He only hid His face occasionally in the Dark Night of the Soul, which some were privileged to endure. We would all undergo it sooner or later, I suggested, and I would wish that he, Mister Simmonds, would say the same things to me, if I came to him in other circumstances. I reminded him of our pledge to one another on the back of the truck that had brought us there: with God's help we would both survive our difficulties, and later on, in the glorious month of August, on the Feast of the Transfiguration, August 6, 1945, we would both make vows together. We would both be happy once again.

84

Billy just looked at me and nodded; he remembered the back of the truck; it was what he had come expecting to hear; it was quite a sermon—my first.

I helped him back to his cell; but before I closed the door, I warned him that, for both our sakes, he should never visit my room again. I said good night and closed the door on him quietly. I had, of course, been severe. But on the whole I had done just fine. Instead of returning directly to my room, however, I made a trip to the john; that way, if anyone noticed I was up, they would expect it to be normal, and not at all suspect that I had been talking with a fellow novice in the middle of the night.

It was a hard time, apparently; Mister Flint left us the next day during work period; we checked and, sure enough, his trunk was gone from the basement. And Mister Kaminsky left a few days later; it was said that he had joined the Marines.

And yet spring did come. I doubt if anywhere in the world there was a more appreciated early spring than that which occurred at Rolling Prairie in 1945: everything burst into green and the prairie came alive with color. The lambs, let out, frolicked, and even old McTavish, the Black Angus bull, when he was let out into the north pasture, as soon as he was free of the five terrified novices who had herded him across the fields, rolled and rubbed himself in the bushes as though he were rolling out of him all the cold confines of the barns and of winter. "He'll have a ball now," said one of the Professed, who was free to speak.

The swallows appeared up in the tower once again;

I didn't notice them coming, they were just there one day, having in them their own good sense of what time of year it was. And we began to feel that we had made it—those of us who were left—that we had survived, and that it would soon be all over. Except for Mister Simmonds, of course, poor old Mister Thirty; yet he, too, was still among us, his voice even more beautiful as he sang us on from Ash Wednesday through Lent and up to Holy Week. And I wondered: had I helped him? Had my words of advice and my loyalty helped him be what he wanted to be? I wondered very much—for by this time everyone seemed to be aware that he was having trouble.

I certainly took things better; nothing on the farm—stenches or sights or the feel of the innards of animals—made me want to retch any more. I was able to laugh at my earlier queasiness; you did get used to everything. Even when Brother Meinrad told me about something called "broadtail lamb" I was not as upset or annoyed as I would have been six months earlier. He called me over to him one afternoon in late February, holding something up that seemed even brighter than the last of the snow which gleamed in the sunlight behind him.

"Look at this, Mister," he said. "Touch it."

I felt it; it seemed incredibly soft, the softest thing I had ever felt. "It's nice," I said. "What is it? Is it fur?"

"It's called broadtail lamb. The reason it's so soft is that the lamb is not allowed to be born. It's taken out of the mother ahead of time, just after it has developed its skin. The Russians started it with a breed of Angora sheep called Karakul. We are trying to do it here with our own breed, trying to get a broadtail operation going."

86

I stared at him. "You mean people actually have a little animal ripped out and killed just for its fleece? I never heard of such a thing!"

Brother Meinrad laughed amiably; he was continuing my education. "I thought you'd like it," he said. "It is rather hard on the mother—actually, it's a bloody mess. But people use it for gloves and things, it's really high fashion. It could mean a lot for the Novitiate, especially during wartime. There is money in it."

I waited to go, but I knew by this time that when Brother Meinrad called me over he always had something else to say that was not connected with what he first spoke about. What was the latest in the war? I wanted to know.

"They've crossed the Rhine into Germany, a place called Remagen. Some traitors didn't blow the bridge up. *Die Verrat!* Treason," he said disgustedly.

Then he said, "Hey—we got our own *kike!*"

I thought for a moment he was speaking again about Mister Simmonds, or about Mister Hanratty, for Meinrad had been angry with him the previous day for going to the infirmary during work period without getting permission. Brother Meinrad had an endless series of Jewish and Yiddish terms—he was really quite educated on the subject—for referring to people he did not like as if they were Jews. "Mister Hanratty?" I asked.

He was annoyed. "*No,* I mean a real Jew. We have a visitor! He was a prisoner in Germany and escaped. You should hear the things he says, I don't believe a word. I'll tell you more later."

The visitor turned out to be Father George Severne, a military chaplain from the British Army. Rumors about him—incredible rumors—swept the Novitiate. It

was variously reported that he had been parachuted into Germany in a commando raid, that he had been in
on the plot to assassinate Hitler, and that he had had to
breathe through a reed underneath the water while the
Nazis searched for him.

None of these turned out to be true, yet the reality of
the man when we finally perceived it was more effective
than if they were. I could not wait to hear him, but, because it was Lent, we would have to wait until Holy
Saturday evening for this sort of diversion. Each novice
knew to the moment when such things happened—that
the long fast and abstinence of Lent were over at noon of
Holy Saturday, that the "Corbonam" or candy press
would be thrown open that afternoon, and that the
earliest time for a welcoming soiree and a talk in Chapel
from Father George would be after supper. But first, all
the grand and triumphant events of Holy Week must
take place.

"Tenebrae factae sunt!" the choir shouted out that
Good Friday evening in the great Feast of Darkness.
Everything else was forgotten in the stupendous service
with its incomparable music which recapitulated the entire story of mankind, from the very beginning even into
the night of the death of the Savior, the voice of God
crying out, "My People, My People! What is there that
I could do that I have not done for you? Like a chosen
vineyard I have planted you and watered you, but thou
wouldst not! *Responde Mihi!"* Reply unto me. Billy was
especially moved by the music which he sang: I could
see his face, he was singing so that he almost became
the words. It became almost unbearable when first the
chapel lights were put out and then each candle of the

seven-branched candlestick was snuffed out by Brother Sacristan, who mounted the altar steps to douse it, to the words of the *Benedictus,* until there was one solitary candle left lighting the entire Chapel, so that it seemed the last flickering light left on earth, and then, in that dramatic Good Friday gesture, it, too, was taken by Brother Sacristan back behind the altar, so that we novices, now a little group of only thirteen young men lost away in the darkness in that tiny place called Rolling Prairie, in that burgeoning spring of 1945, felt that we were all left totally in gloom—without light, without Christ, without God, it seemed, as indeed it was supposed to seem. It was as if Billy was singing us all away, far away from the world; it was as though the voice of Billy had become the flickering tongue of flame, so that when it disappeared behind the altar I actually felt apprehension that it had gone out, that Billy himself had met his end.

"Illumine those who sit in darkness, and in the shadow of death," the psalm concluded, the choir shouting to a crescendo, "and direct instead their feet into the way of peace!" The candle was brought back, in silence, and the tension was over. Suddenly a wild explosion of noise thundered through the Chapel as though a bomb had gone off: it was only the choir slamming their books shut, as monks have done from time immemorial, but the huge tomes closing upon themselves, sounding like the clap of doom and the bursting open of the earth, left us all giggling and snickering embarrassedly when the lights were turned on. The novices were astonished; but the wise old ones among us, the Professed, were left smiling in their knowledge of how things were done.

*   *   *

And so on Good Friday there was death; everything died with Christ. All and each of us felt death in us. The statues were covered with purple cloth and had been since Palm Sunday. No bell or musical instrument was sounded from Maundy Thursday on—the piano lid in the recreation room was put down over the keys, and Mister Coon, the organist, quietly folded down the cover over the great Chapel organ. For the only time in the year even old Augustine was silenced and stopped ringing out to us how late the hour was and how much later it was than when we first believed.

I, too, as Regulator ceased ringing life on; my small bell was silenced: instead I was given a ridiculous wooden clapper that everybody snickered at when I first tried to use it. All other sound had gone out except the sound of human voices mourning to God over death. Nowhere was death more evident than in the Chapel itself. The Tabernacle door lay open: there was nothing in it. The Tabernacle—the tent, literally, that God had pitched among us, in which the manna from heaven had been stored—lay empty. The Veil of the Temple was rent from top to bottom, as though God had left His Temple, as though God had abandoned His Chosen People, as though God had abandoned Man.

We lived the events of Holy Week more than sang them; we had prepared many months for it, so that the Last Supper and the Washing of the Feet and the kiss of Judas and the cutting off of the ear of the high priest's servant all became more real than the events of the day; the ordinary actual happenings of the week of March 25, 1945, in the rest of the world, and the life of the farm, were by contrast somehow less real. We were exhausted from it, and our Roman collars hung on us like the harnesses that you saw on the great dray animals in the barns.

And yet it was not all finished. That year Father Master granted permission for a liturgical experiment. Instead of the Blessing of the New Fire as it was traditionally done at dawn of Holy Saturday, we were to have it as a late-night vigil for Easter.

Thus we celebrated the end of Lent earlier in the evening, with a full meal—the first since Ash Wednesday. Afterward, at a soiree, the Corbonam was opened and we were given candy, too, for the first time in six weeks. For all our pursuit of perfection, we were still young men, and our lack of self-control came out on such occasions. Mister Reedy, who remained large and fat in spite of all his fasting, asked us ahead of time to keep him from "making a pig" of himself; nevertheless he had to be physically restrained by his friend Mister Carsten, to the inevitable amused cries of "Greedy Reedy!" from all over the recreation room.

It was into this mood of celebration that Father George Severne came. When it was explained to him what was happening, he laughed politely and said in a pronounced British accent, "The Corbonam? Well, you young men have got quite a novel name for your candy press, I must say!"

As things quieted and the candy disappeared, Father George was introduced. Father Master began by saying that he would not have us ignorant, that he was not known to let young men pass out from his tutelage "wet behind the ears"; consequently, when the opportunity arose to have someone such at Father George speak to us of the experience of the Church and its priesthood in difficult areas, he felt it incumbent upon him to invite the visitor to address us and to share with us some of his wisdom and experience. He then yielded to Father George.

Father George thanked him, remarked that any comments of his would possess more experience than any wisdom that he was aware of, and he asked us what it was we were most interested in hearing.

Some wanted to hear about the war, and when it would end, but Father George said he did not know when it would end and that the only part he had been in had been North Africa, which was now part of history. Mister Knous then shouted, "Your escape, tell us about your escape!"

" I had best tell you something about life in the camps, first. Lindenfels is in the Schwarzwald," he said. "It is on the Romantischestrasse—the Route of the Old German Heroes. Siegfried passed that way on his Rhineland journeys." Father George immediately struck me as an educated man, one who perhaps had read history and attended great operas; a vague yearning to be such a man tinged my spirit as he spoke. "Lindenfels, in fact, in more than one way reminds me of your place here, for though it is certainly more hilly than Rolling Prairie, still the pine forest you have up on your Hill of Calvary makes it seem the same. But the air is much cleaner here. . . ." He looked at us for a moment, as though he might be wondering how much of his experience it would be good for us to hear. He turned to Father Master and asked, "Father Master, perhaps there are some things you would prefer the novices should not hear? Perhaps I ought not to tell too much about life or death in the camps?"

Father Master bridled; we all knew that one of his

main themes was that we were all developing into mature adults. Moreover, in my talks with Meinrad, I had heard what his views were on the war; they were the views of the Reverend Charles Coughlin, the ones that I had been raised on: that the war had been brought about by the International Bankers and the Jews, and that America had no business being involved with foreign entanglements.

Instead of losing his temper, however, Father Master simply turned to Father George and said, "These men know what time of day it is," nodding in our direction. "It is unlikely anything you have to say will shock them. Proceed."

Father Severne shook his head thoughtfully. Then he began. "They're burning people, you know. The main difference between Lindenfels, as I have said, and your lovely place here is the quality of the air: at Lindenfels the sky during the day has a sickly brown pallor hanging over it, depending on which way the wind is blowing. At night there is always an overcast which lights up from time to time from the constantly burning furnaces. And every day, as you grow weaker at work and have less to eat, you know that you are closer and closer to the furnace yourself and that one day you will be gone up the chimney or lighting the night sky. It is difficult to be charitable, or to regard *anyone* as your neighbor, under such circumstances.

"Nevertheless, in that hell I did find one man who was a neighbor, one man who still managed to be kind. His name was Mordecai—I never got his last name. He was a Jew, from Poland, I think. People are numbers in the camps, not names, and he wore a number and *Der Gelbe Stern*—the yellow Star of David—always over the right

93

back shoulder. The SS pinned it on prisoners as though they were animals stamped for meat approval.

"It was terrible. The dogs went for the genitals if you tried to escape. Women with child coming into the camps were shot, the child dying in the womb unborn. The Germans were getting short on things, you know, and a pregnant woman is just a burden, she cannot work, and she takes up food. All children under a certain age were marched right off the trains to grave ditches in the forest; we knew it; they had to dig their own graves first, take off their clothes, and then fall, naked, into the earth. Most of them were Jews, though some were 'slave nationalities' from the rest of Europe also. I was captured as a legitimate prisoner of war in North Africa in 1941, and for a while was treated as a prisoner of war according to the rule of Geneva. But after a while, because I did not answer questions properly or perhaps asked too many, I ended up in the camps like everybody else, and for all practical purposes was treated as a Jew myself."

As I listened, I became conscious of mutterings or mumblings behind me, several pews back. At first I thought someone might be having trouble holding back laughter about some irrelevancy, and I was afraid that Mister Jenkins' inevitable nervous guffaw might break loose, but the disturbance was coming from too far back in the Chapel for that. I realized it was from among the Professed Brothers, and then of course I knew what was going on: Brother Meinrad would be making a running commentary on everything the English priest was saying. I knew by heart what it would include—that the war was England's war, that Hitler had been forced into it, that the Treaty of Versailles was unjust, and so on. Every so often in his delivery Father George would look up and pause, until he turned to Father Master and said, "Someone seems to be having some sort of difficulty—I wonder if there is a question I might answer?"

At once Brother Meinrad shot to his feet. I could see him out of the corner of my eye. He was standing with his hands on the pew in front of him like some American patriot from a painting, a "Give Me Liberty or Give Me Death" stance, or like a prisoner in the dock about to make a heroic last speech.

"Yes, Brother?" Father Master asked.

Indignantly Brother asked what truth there could possibly be in the assertions that the Germans had committed anything worse than what was common to all wars; indeed, the British and the Americans were in reality doing the same things and worse, only Churchill and Roosevelt did not let us know. Brother Meinrad asked Father George (for a question it was more like a speech) for specifics: what precisely did the Nazis do that was any worse than what the Russian Communists were doing to German boys on the Eastern Front? And what of Mister Roosevelt's cooperating with them in foreign meeting after foreign meeting? What was it that they did, he screamed, that made them so bad?

For a long time Father George did not speak. Then he said simply, "They used people like meat—the SS hung them up on hooks while they were still alive and their hearts still pounding."

Brother Meinrad was briefly taken aback, but only briefly. He paused, and took a deeper breath. "What I want to know is, is that something you *heard* about and are now telling us like it was the Gospel truth or is this something you saw and were present for? *All I ask is to know:* to understand what it is that has been done wrong. What did they do?"

There was so much confusion at this point that a guffaw came from Mister Jenkins, which we all knew by this late date in the year only happened at moments of extreme tension and was not really laughing at all. Yet, when I heard it, I was afraid that uncontrolled giggling might occur.

Father George controlled the situation. "Brother," he said in a kind voice, "I know that as you are a Religious it may be impossible to believe that mankind would act this way. And I know that as you are obviously German and I am English it may be equally as difficult to believe that I am being objective about things. And so I will simply tell you one incident which I was present for—and I was *indeed* present for it—which should be sufficient.

"The man in charge of Lindenfels was Felix Fromm, a general of the SS, and a staunch Roman Catholic. But he was mad; he was insane—or perhaps deliberately appeared to be—on the subject of butterflies."

There was another pause, and I cringed in my pew lest someone would titter.

" 'Butterfly-collecting is not slight!' he would shout at us, as though we cared. He must have been a professor in civilian life, or else that is what he wanted to be. He would stand us up and give us long lectures—after work when we were exhausted—about how all things could be seen even in the small wings of a butterfly were we but sensitive enough to observe. 'Man is not worthy of the butterfly!' he would shout. *'Die Schmetterling!'* He would tell us this in German, and then in English, and in a half a dozen other languages, for he was fluent. 'My friends,' he would say, 'observe them when they fly through our camp: in the fall they are—*peregrinus*—how do you say, pilgrims?—to the far and distant deserts of Africa, across the Mittelsee. Then in spring, like the birds, they fly across the Pyrenees, the Alps, through here, on the way to La Manche, to England, and to the Hebrides.'

"He was entranced, captivated; even in our exhausted state we knew that he knew his business, that he was intoxicated with his subject, totally entranced by it. And so he would make us stand, hour after hour, for his lectures. He told us everything, better I am sure than many university professors, and I am certain that had I been in something approaching a human condition I would have been enlightened by wisdom concerning one of God's lesser creatures, the entire genus of Lepidoptera.

"But, my dear men, we were not—we were most horrendously not—in a state remotely resembling a human condition, or what you hear these days referred to as 'a proper learning environment.' Fromm was sick; he was sicker than we were. He kept us standing there in the hot sun or the cold rain or, often, snow, telling us about butterflies, their wings and their habits—to us who cared for nothing but to get inside and stop standing and gain some nourishment.

"Why? For one reason: it all had to do with escaping. The man's mad mind was filled with only one thought: that we would escape, that even one of us would get away, away from the dogs, past the barbed wire and the searchlights. He was Felix Fromm, you see, general of the Third Reich and of the SS, and the security of Lindenfels was his grave responsibility. All the talk about butter-

97

flies was to torment us into a perpetual, final, and frozen fear, to keep us from ever even thinking about escape.

"And yet Mordecai—my friend—did, or, that is, he tried.

"Mordecai was a sensitive, kind person, even in the hideousness of the camp. I greatly admired his religious faith, his sense of humor even in all the happenings of Lindenfels. Instead of shoes, he wore a pair of rubbers which he had saved from somewhere, and though he joked about them, they were actually his prize possessions, for they protected him against the slush and offal that was everywhere. He once pulled me aside and told me that if anything ever happened to him, I should consider them his gift to me. When I protested and asked why he was so thoughtful, Mordecai whispered simply, in his broken way of speaking English, 'I try to help my next.' I had to ask him to repeat it before I realized he meant he tried to help his neighbor—I was his 'next.'

"He used to pray at night. I could not understand the mixture of languages that he spoke, but I knew the Scripture well enough to catch snatches of Isaiah, Elias, Jeremiah. The one I always knew, for I felt like saying it with him, was Elias' great complaint about God. 'You have duped me, O Lord; I am become an object of laughter, all the day the word of the Lord has brought me reproach. I say to myself, I will not mention Him, I will speak His name no more.'

"Poor Mordecai! They were among the last words out of him. He was caught trying to escape in the night.

"Next morning Fromm announced a lecture of supreme importance: we were to see our first Red Butterfly! One had been caught, in camp! The collection would be enriched by a most exquisite specimen."

98

Father George stopped, clearly considering one more time if he should go on. "Look here—I did not come to intrude upon your beautiful celebration here, the observance of Holy Week which you are all doing so well; within the walls of a Novitiate I hesitate to mention what happened. Moreover, many of you are young people, deserving of special consideration.

"And yet you also deserve to hear, and the world deserves to hear, the worst. You cannot shut your ears—no man can and still call himself a man—cannot shut your ears to what has happened among us. The thing must be said by somebody, must be listened to by someone—if not by an infinite, merciful God, then at least by poor, fallible, frightened man."

Father Master nodded to something of what had been said.

"We were hauled out after work period; nothing was sacred enough to excuse us from work period. Fromm was there as Herr Professor with all his talk about *die Kunst, die Aufgabe,* and *der Nachtfalter, die Raupe.* Mordecai, caught, was brought out and held between two SS men like some guilty student standing in front of the classroom about to be made a dunce in the corner. After what seemed about two hours of endless chatter and nonsense about how fine the collection was, including doubtless some very real and valuable knowledge about the genus Lepidoptera which, had we been anything but starving, exhausted prisoners, might have interested us, Fromm rapped his baton sharply on his lectern. He flipped it like a wand in the direction of the prisoner, and four more SS men came up, armed with equipment.

"It was . . . odd equipment. There were ropes and various irons—a buzz saw, which I took to be for putting up a scaffolding, so that for a moment I thought there was going to be a hanging or even that we were to witness a crucifixion scene.

"It was worse.

"I will get this over as quickly as possible. What was done was that the prisoner was spread-eagled, roughly and very tautly, his arms pulled and pinioned to stakes, his legs to other stakes, until his body was taut and he could not move. An SS made two cuts in his back beneath the two shoulderblades. Another SS came up with the cutting saw. He then cut through the bones, several ribs on each side, as though the human being in front of him were some farm animal instead of a man. I still could not conceive of what they were up to; how could anyone have thought in that direction? A third SS man, a butcher of a person, then reached in with the aid of a cruel grappling instrument and extracted each of the prisoner's lungs, so that, still breathing, still functioning, they lay out flat upon the back. Then, under Fromm's scrupulous scrutiny, they were carefully arranged out into their full form.

"At last he was satisfied. 'The Red Butterfly, my friends,' Fromm said. 'It is very rare, I am sure you will have to admit. I want you to look at it closely. Study it, the movement of its wings. *Die Schmetterling!*'

"For hours, how many I do not know, we were compelled to stand at attention. I do not know whether Mordecai was conscious or not, or whether he had been unconscious from the beginning. He did live for some time, though; the cruel evidence of his waning life was terribly clear. I felt that he died sometime within the first half-hour. I wondered what he thought now, or if he was capable of thought. And as I stood there, his last words kept repeating themselves in my brain: 'I say to myself, I will not mention Him, I will speak his name no more. . . .'

" 'My next,' I thought. 'My poor next.' "

"After it got dark—it must have been well past eleven at night—Fromm returned, spoke some more of *Die Aufgabe*, and released us. As we broke ranks to return to barracks, on legs that could hardly move, I managed to pass close by the dead body of my friend. I saw his two rubbers strewn beneath him where they had fallen when the guards had raised him. I reached down, with terrible pain; I picked them up, his last heritage to me.

"The next day, weak as I was, I escaped. I saw a chance, and slipped under the electrified wire at the ditch near the septic tanks at the end of the camp. I was wearing my friend's rubbers—they were better than what I had had on my feet; and, you know, I think I may have owed my life to them: the bloodhounds were out, I heard them often during my trip, but they never came close to me, and I think maybe they were following the wrong scent, that the rubbers were not what they had been set to follow.

"I succeeded in leaving the Lindenfels area. I ate acorns and certain small clumps of vegetation. I got sick on food often, and yet it was better than in camp. Once I stole some eggs from a German farm. I headed south, toward what I hoped was the Swiss border. Over the next forty days I wandered. I climbed first through the Oden-wald; I remember places with names like Sternenfels, Todtmoos, Schounau. I actually crossed over into Switzerland apparently above a place called Sackingen, and did not know I was free, and was afraid to ask. I only felt that I must head for the Alps, and the biggest line of mountains I could see was of course the Jura, but I had no maps.

"I felt very much at home in the Jura. The plant life reminded me of my native England—saxifrage, bedstraws, and speedwells looked out at me from the rocks. But most of all, I saw flying rapidly that most British of butterflies, the Painted Lady! I knew all about them from Fromm— even their Latin name: *Vanessa Cardui*. I knew they bred on the edges of the Sahara, and that they would be flying north at that time of the year, coming down from the Alpine passes to find their way to England—only, of course, they were going backward, for my purposes, toward Lindenfels! I even found time to laugh at them, for they seemed as anxious to get to Fromm's butterfly farm as I was to leave it. I used to lecture them, while following their path the other way in my rubbers: 'Be careful, Vanessa;' I would say. 'Be careful, little one—you will end up in the Commander's Collection!'

"By following their route, I actually climbed over the Schweize Jura, through one of the lower passes; I collapsed by a road outside the town of Aarburg, and awoke in a Swiss hospital.

"That was only one year ago."

After Father Severne got to that point, he decided to stop, as though he had gone on long enough. Father Master seemed pleased that the talk was over; he asked if anyone had any questions. I turned in my seat and looked at Brother Meinrad; he looked weary, as though exhausted in the effort to communicate with this Englishman. He arose, and in that patient tone some people use when talking to children he said, "The Germans are a loving people. Do you know the word *Gemüt-*

lichkeit? There is no word for it in the English language. It means a feeling of humanity, of the Soul. Schiller had it. Brahms and Beethoven had it. That is why the Germans love music. '*Seid umschlangen, Millionen!* You millions, I embrace you!' they sing. Now, how can they be so bad!"

Father Severne said something to the effect that he could not answer that, that he could only tell what he had seen.

"Then they were betrayed," Brother said, and sat sadly back in his seat.

I began to fear it would all be over before I understood it. I felt myself rising, and I heard my voice, hoarse as it usually is when I am nervous, speaking. "Father Severne," I heard it say, "why did you risk such a terrible death by trying to escape? How could you possibly have found the courage to even think of such a thing?"

The answer was simple and matter of fact: "It is the duty of a British officer to escape in time of war; it is written into the Manual of Arms."

I was astonished by the answer, but there was no more time for questions; the Easter Vigil was about to begin, and Father Master urged us all to move quickly to the Chapel for it.

The Feast of Light is really the high point of the Church's Liturgy. Light is kindled from flint sparks upon strands of flax, and the lighted candle signifying Christ the Savior is brought up the darkened main aisle. The celebrant calls out three times the words *"Lumen Christi!"*; the congregation genuflects in adoration and calls back, *"Deo Gratias!"*

The *Exultet* follows, springing from the mind of

mighty Augustine of Hippo, and put to plainchant by the High Middle Ages; in it, creation itself is said to exult that the long night of sin and darkness is over, that man's loneliness of enmity with God and with himself is at last finished, ended by the arrival at last of the long-awaited Redeemer. "This is the night," it shouts. "This, then, is the night of the ancient Paschal rites, wherein the true Lamb is slain, with whose blood the doorposts of the People of God are consecrated. . . . This is the night on which Thou didst cause our fathers, the Children of Israel, to cross dry-shod the Red Sea, leading them out of the bondage of the Land of Egypt. . . . This, then, is the night which has purged away the darkness of sins with the illumination of the Pillar of Fire. . . . O wondrous condescension! O inestimable affection! Oh, *happy* fault, which brought about so glorious a Savior!"

Mister Simmonds sang the words remarkably well: "*O vere beata nox, quae exspoliavit Aegyptios, ditavit Hebraeos!*" He more than sang them, he became them, to such an extent that, knowing what I did about his problems, I wondered where it would end with him.

It is a strange thing; many people cannot say exactly where they were on a given date, in World War II or anywhere else, once the moment has receded from memory; but for some of us, certain dates will never be forgotten; they refuse to recede from memory. I know where I was on the night of March 31: I was with my brothers at Rolling Prairie, Indiana, singing the Easter Vigil. It was the night my friend died.

After that, however, my memory is not a reliable record. I have some memory, or is it imagination, that Billy came to me again, speaking Latin. He was full of "*Hora venit*'s" and "*Quare fremuit*'s" and "*sunt inanias*'s" and other things which I did not understand. The hour was late and I was asleep. "Go back to bed, I will speak to you in the morning," I said drowsily but firmly and closed the door.

My sleep was vexed to nightmare and sickness, and I was in the infirmary up next to the Chapel tower; I must have passed in and out of consciousness, the big bell interfering with my rest. I heard it saying all sorts of things to me: that Billy was dead and that others were dead, that it was late and that it was night and that I was sleeping when I should be awake and that I should get up to awaken the others and that I had failed and that my faith was vain and that the Tabernacle was empty and that Father George was escaping and that God had lied.

All day long in the bright sunshine of the infirmary bed I lay up close to Augustine in his bell tower. All through the bright, hot, warming days of that spring of 1945 the huge voice boomed out above me that it was night, and I, who had eyes to see the bright light of day with, looked out and could not see; for the voice kept telling me it was night and that True Midnight had already occurred and, oh, it was terrible, and that the swallows were gone and that Father George had escaped and did not believe and, *going out, he hanged himself* and it was *he that put his hand with me in the dish* and the great vats steaming and the entrails and the blood. And the voice repeated how you had to toughen yourself up for everything and be a priest forever. Delirium and temperature 104° in the heat outside the empty Tabernacle in the desert with Bedouins and camels and *who owns our bodies* and the flutterwings of the butterfly,

the Red Butterfly, the *Schmetterling*, he called it, cruci-
fied spread-eagled above them and an escape in rubbers
over the mountains to Switzerland, and it stopped. But
then it would start again and I heard the great, clanking
chain mechanisms of Augustine winding up to tell me
again the day and the hour.

Sometimes, too, there were funeral bells and the
Chorus Angelorum and the *Ego Sum* of Job of the march
to the cemetery, and the hump of sod in the soil of the
prairie, the clay. Adam, clay: man, all humans, death
and work and bells and time. And I fell back asleep and
it started over again, that it was *millesimo*, that it was
nongentesimo, that it was *quadragesimo*, that it was
quarto. *Quarto?* No, what came after *quarto* was *quinto*,
the Year of Our Lord, and my year, too.

"Good morning, Mister!" It was the sternly happy
voice of Mister Skeffington, the infirmarian, with a breakfast of tea and toast. I was better. Better of something
that I had had. I was getting well. I was no longer Regulator—that job had been thought too demanding for someone in my condition. Father Master had indicated instead
that a little rest was necessary and soon I would be all
right.

Father George was all right, too, I slowly learned, only
he was someplace else. But it was some time before I
learned that Billy was not all right and that that part of
my dreams was true, that he was dead, and that Father
Master had publicly announced that it was not suicide
because the man was in no condition to be responsible
for his own death, that he had been overwrought. But it
was a very long time later that anyone would tell me
anything about how he died: that he had hanged himself

on Holy Saturday night out in the barn. I had slept in the next morning and for the first time all year had failed to wake the house up on time, and it was then they discovered something was wrong with me and sent me to the infirmary to rest.

"You gave us quite a time of it," said Mister Skeffington, smiling. "One morning you went running through the main corridor ringing the bell and shouting, 'It is midnight! It is midnight! True Midnight has already occurred!' You were right, too, of course; it was two o'clock in the morning!"

I do remember some things. The death of President Roosevelt; the deaths of Mussolini and Hitler and prayers of thanksgiving that the city of Rome and the life of the Holy Father had been spared in the war. Then VE Day, and the war over in Europe, at least.

After that, the spring hurried by and turned quickly into summer. I was allowed out to work again, only in the fields now, doing good, hard work that repaired me. For a while I worried whether I would be allowed to be professed on time, but Father Master told me that I worried about too many things; he pronounced me fine and a perfect candidate for the religious life and the vows. By June it was as though nothing had happened, and my life at the Novitiate had returned to normal. Father Master called me in for Monitions in early July and told me I should prepare myself to take vows on August 6, the Feast of the Transfiguration of Our Lord, with the other members of my class, who now numbered eleven, the others having departed.

Profession Day finally did arrive. The day dawned with a brightness the world had never seen. Looking out my window, I saw that the prairie was beautiful, and off toward the west rose little fluffy clouds—fair-weather clouds, I knew, far, far beyond the town of Rolling Prairie; it would be a good day.

Later I recited my vows. I was nervous and could not at first sign my name, my hand was shaking so. And I needed help with the cincture: Mister Lawson kindly helped tie me. The Latin was difficult, but eventually I, too, along with eleven others, I too got to my ending, to the *"Millesimo nongentesimo quadragesimo quinto"* of August 6 of the Year of Our Lord 1945. After it was over, Father Master in the Sacristy reached over and our hands clasped in a firm, manly gesture of fraternal unity.

There is not much more to say. We spent, as was the custom, one week more at the Novitiate to lead the next class into their year. And during the week we worked, in silence, at the same old jobs we had done before we were professed. One afternoon during the week, however, as I was reporting into the subkitchen to help can tomatoes and other fruits in season, Brother Just pulled me over to the side to tell me something. "They've dropped a big bomb on Japan. It's called an atom bomb. My brother sent me a card: he said the heat from the bomb was so great it seared the bottom of the plane, and it flipped the plane over three times!"

So that was it. That was the reason for the big bombers, the B29's I had noticed flying over the Novitiate during the entire Novitiate year, with their high, high tails and long, deadly noses. So much had happened in the world while we were on the prairie. "The war will soon be over," Brother Just continued. "They probably have more of them." I nodded and turned to the vegetables with a feeling of guilt—for having broken silence with a fellow novice.

The last day was August 14, the eve of the Feast of the Assumption of Our Blessed Lady as Queen of Heaven. Father Mulloughney, a noted liturgist, took as his texts for a lengthy talk a collage of quotations from the liturgy both for the Feast of the Assumption of the Blessed Virgin as Queen of Heaven and quotes from the Feast of the Transfiguration of Jesus a week earlier, whose octave we were celebrating. He ingeniously wove them together with the history of the day, in such a way that the Sacred Scriptures themselves seemed to have foretold what had happened in the skies over Hiroshima eight days before: "And He was transfigured before them," Father Mulloughney quoted. "His face shone as the Sun, and His vestments were as white as snow. A blinding flash illuminated the East, and the Earth shook in its tracks!" he shouted. Then he moved on to the day's feast: "Who is this that ascends like the dawn into the heavens? Beautiful as the moon, shining as the sun, terrible as an army in battle array?" He went on to show that the world was in its latter days, that there were unmistakable signs upon the heavens that Christ's Second Coming was imminent.

Knowing our ignorance, Father Mulloughney brought us up to date with things. A powerful bomb, called an atomic bomb, had been dropped on Japan, at a place called Hiroshima, something more powerful than the world had ever seen. It had turned that city into a pyre of immense magnitude. Half a million people had been estimated dead. Reports emanating from the doomed country of the enemy described people losing their eyes in the first fraction of a second. Some, closer to what was called "Zero Point," were totally vaporized in the terrible, fiery holocaust. Outlines of human beings—what were once human beings—were visible, it was said, in the sidewalks where they had been standing. There was no question that the world had entered upon a new age, and little question that man was in the final stages of human history.

He closed by congratulating the newly professed, and urged us to develop a life of dedication to the Queen of Heaven, in order to bring God's mercy to the People of God. I thought the talk remarkable, but wished that I would get more information on the subject than was possible through a sermon.

Later in the morning of August 14, my last day—toward high noon, in fact—I went up to Calvary for one last look out over the prairie and all that it had meant to me, and all that had happened while I had been there. I felt exuberant, a quiet sense that I had conquered myself and had won out in the end. I stood there looking out upon God's world with a sense of hard-won peace. I prayed for different things, looking out into the distance, remembering especially all those who had vowed their lives with me that day, and trying to remember all those who were no longer with us. I could hear the sounds of the farm and could see everything. Brother Meinrad was bringing the truck up to the Novitiate building, and the men were assembling to get on. Suddenly there was a sound of another engine, louder than the truck, and I looked up to see a fighter plane rapidly approaching. The sound became exciting, rising in pitch as it got closer, and I recognized the plane as a P-47 Thunderbolt. The pilot must have caught sight of the solitary figure in black upon the little hillock, and he came roaring down right over me, so near that I could even see his grinning face, his two fingers pointing up in Churchill's "V for Victory," and two long rows of Swastikas painted underneath the cockpit window: he was an "ace"—he had clearly shot down enough in combat for that.

Now, years later, I know what I did not know then: that that morning the world was celebrating VJ Day, that the war was over, not only in Europe but in Japan. The young man was celebrating, with Rolling Prairie and anybody else who wanted to, the victory of freedom.

I alone seemed not to know, and not even to surmise, what was happening. I went down the hill toward the truck to get in line with those who were waiting. I looked up at the tower and saw old Augustine, without the swallows. After I got in line, I whispered something to the man standing next to me. "Judas Priest," I said, "—Judas K. Priest." But he was staring off into the distance and either did not hear me or did not want to. *"Bruder!"* I heard the voice inside me saying, and *"Welt!"* for no apparent reason. The truck was ready, to take us closer to priesthood, closer to the white linen binding anointed hands, closer to being hidden with Christ, to the one thing that was necessary. First our suitcases were tossed onto the truck and tied securely with heavy farm ropes so that they could not escape; then we got on ourselves, all that was left of us, the eleven others and I; the piece of fencing that served as a tailgate was lifted into position and fastened. There were some cheers, and Brother Meinrad turned the heavy wheels out into the farm lane, down past the various barns, which were busy as usual, between fields of ripening grain, and finally out, beyond the last of the barbed-wire fences to the highway, the open road, taking us on to what came next, to four years of Philosophy at Notre Dame, then on to what it was really all about: to the House of Dogmatic Theology in Washington, where we would learn the Sacred Dogmas of the Church, study the ways of God with Man, and make of our lives a Holocaust of Divine Love.

☒ *CHORUS . . . . .*

*My friend the Letter Writer—Anonymous, she who
can do nothing, she who thinks nothing can be done—I
must not neglect her. . . .*

*Sometimes I am fierce with her. "Anonymous!" I cry.
"Full inquiry! We must find a name for you!"*

*She is like me. She says she was born free—do you
believe that? And she does not have enough faith. Thinks
of suicide. God must have a reason. She loved her Chapel
—there was no place like that.*

*Next, you seem to be me, back then. Are you not me,
then?*

Riddle!

We are all Nexts: it is myself I seek.

*   *   *

But Semblable, *what is your answer? "And by op-posing, end them"?*
None? Nothing? You will do nothing?

I understand. Admit me Chorus to this history.

Lonely House Now

I pray thee, do not mock me, fellow student.
Hamlet I, ii, 177

I. Outside the Choir

" 'Error has no rights!' Gentlemen,—'*Error—has—no—rights!'*—What, Gentlemen, does Holy Mother Church mean when She states that '*Error has no rights*'?" The great voice of the Reverend Daniel E. Corkery boomed out the question three times, just as it had repeated every such question through four years in Washington; it hung over our heads and wound its way up into the far corners of the Aula Magna: the Lecture Hall of Sacred and Dogmatic Theology.

Father Corkery always reminded me of a great bull sent to torment us each year at our college in the Nation's capital, eyes staring, nostrils snorting and hooves pawing, asking, "Gentlemen? Gentlemen?" over and over while deciding which one of us to devour. I did not get along with him. "You do not believe," he had said. "You have a look on your face in class that you are not accepting what is being taught."

My head was prudently held down that day; I had been drawing in the margin of my Dogma notes. I was drawing a Navy F9F Pantherjet taking off from the deck of a carrier. There was just barely room for it, however, alongside the tract *De Novissimis,* for higher in the margin was a Lockheed Super-G Constellation which I had drawn earlier.

"Gentlemen?" The roar of the voice made me turn quickly to an empty page and think rapidly, in case my name should be called, of words in which to put the concept, to fend off the tormentor so that I might get through to ordination, get ordained safely and be free of him, free of all this, out of the Aula, a grown-up man and a priest of God forever, which was all I really wanted.

It was a most severe concept, however, that error had no right, and one most difficult to put into words. First you had to point out that the Roman Catholic Church, as the one true church, founded by Christ upon the Rock of Peter and Peter's successors the Popes, possessed, alone, God's Truth revealed to Man. Next you had to show how only those things which had existence *themselves* could possess anything else. Only then did it become clear that Error, which as Falsehood did not enjoy existence itself, could not possess anything else, either, and could not— *a fortiori*—ever be said to possess any rights. You had to cite the proper text, *"Extra Ecclesiam Christi, nulla salus."* And, finally, before you were finished, you had to apply it to all those who professed error, and, of course, to the erring human individual himself, whose condition was, necessarily, severe.

Father Corkery turned in his chair and looked sideways toward each corner of the Aula Magna; his gaze followed a path which took in every semicircle of benches, up to the top of the amphitheater, over, and then back down. For a moment it rested on me; but then the voice said, "Mister Schunermann!" I relaxed, with all those who had escaped.

"—Mister Schunermann—" said Father Corkery in an exaggeratedly courteous tone, "—Would you care to elucidate for us? What do we mean when we say that Error *can* have no rights?"

Schuney's corpulent behind squirmed painfully on the seat in front of me.

He faced an impossible task. I knew that before they were finished, Father Corkery would insist on being taken Thesis by Thesis, Corollary by Corollary, Scholion by Scholion, up and down all thirty-two levels of the great *Schema Censurae.* This was the vast and complicated outline of the binding force assigned by theologians to every level of what was to be believed, as well as the proscribing force of each Anathema, all the way from Error itself, or True Heresy formally condemned in Council, down through lesser faults called "Proximate to Heresy," down to simple Confusion and Ignorance— divided into "invincible" and "supine"—mistakes unworthy of special consideration. Altogether, it was the grand summation of everything that Father Corkery taught us; it was on a chart labeled "Denziger & Co." rolled up behind the Chair, its string dangling down over the blackboard.

"Perhaps—if the question is too large—you could apply it specifically for us to the tract under discussion, *De Novissimis?* What Heresy is historically connected with the Last Rites of the Church, with Extreme Unction, the Sacrament of the Dying? What infamous heretical sect wrongly taught that there was no need for Last Anointing, and rejected the consolations of the Church?" He made a little pawing movement on the lectern, and I could see his cane, with its ivory head, starting its move toward the blackboard.

He was referring to the Albigensians, I knew, the Cathari of southern France. They had rejected the Last Rites of the Church, even on their deathbeds, preferring to face death without it. Pope Benedict XIII, after years of trying to save them, had had to hand them over at last to "the Secular Arm," under the great Christian general Simon de Montfort, who attacked them in their hillside towns, sealed them up in caves, and burned them alive. The only ones to escape were the mothers and children, who hurled themselves off the cliffs rather than submit to Rome. I knew all this well enough; I had memorized the answer for many an examination.

Schunermann had got only three words out when Father Corkery threw his head back and rolled his eyes in disbelief. "Mister Schunermann!" he said. "I fear you are *Manichean* this morning!" Amusement at Schunermann being Manichean circled through the class; Father Corkery was in one of his rare playful moods. He tossed to the winds everything that Schuney managed to say: "Oh, Mister Schunermann—now you are being *Nestorian* on the matter!" and "Are you a *Lutheran?*" Finally, when Father Corkery in a loud voice said, "Richard, you are positively *Priscillian!*" the class broke up in laughter, and Schunermann himself laughed at being caught in so many heresies. Father Corkery leaned back in his chair, grasping the chart-cord; *"Extra choram cantat,* Gentle-men—*Extra—choram—cantat,"* he said—'He sings outside the choir.' What choir? The choir of orthodox theologians of the Church!" And with that he rolled down the great *Schema Censurae.*

He went to the board and, rapping robustly, said "In ascending order: Levels of Belief. The lowest level: *Sententia Communior*—mere opinion, albeit the learned opinion of devout and holy men. We are obliged to respect it, though it is one among at least several."

"Second level: *Sententia Communis."* Again the cane rap. *"The* single commonly held opinion, held in common by all Catholic theologians. The Theological Note attached to it is not without some binding force, as you shall see. . . .

"Third, *De Fide Definita:* a doctrine enunciated by the Teaching Magisterium of the Church, of such binding force that to oppose it implies the risk of Heresy. Do not underestimate this category, Gentlemen. . . .

"And finally, at the very top, we have *De Fide Divina et Cattolica*—the article of Faith which exists both in Sacred Scripture and which has also been defined as such by one of the Ecumenical Councils of the Church—the Holy Father himself acting in unison with the fathers of the Universal Church; this, Gentlemen, is True Dogma, *that Divine and Catholic faith which it is incumbent upon every man born into this world to accept in the depths of his being,* which he rejects at his own peril, unless overcome by what is known as Invincible Ignorance—the 'Unconquerable Ignorance' of the stupid and foolish."

He strode across the room to the left side. *"Haeretice*

stricte"—a rap against the board—*"Haeretice Proxima . . ."* and on down the list he went, until he came to the last one, at the bottom.

"And here, Gentlemen, we have the last, pitiful form of Error which theologians have bothered to give a name to, an item called "Offensive to Pious Ears"—though, I must say, it *loses* something in the translation!"

As he began to drone on about *Sententia Communis* and *Minus Probabilis*, he appeared safely fixed in his track for the morning, and so I discreetly turned back the pages of my notebook, back before the Lockheed Constellation, before the Mustangs and Corsairs and all the fighter planes, back to the first drawing, to drawing number one: my chalice.

Everyone drew chalices. You spent the four years of theology drawing yours, since each man designed his own. The four years of theology were four years of visits from chalice salesmen, up in the magnificent front parlors. "Beaugrand is here," someone would shout, "Beaugrand of Canada!" and we would all rush up to see the salesman taking off the swaddling from a hundred samples of stunning craftsmanship. Or it was Hammer of Baltimore, or Des Clee of Belgium, or even Domgoldschmiedehaus of Trier, in the Rhineland. They all produced masterful work, and you spent your life trying to incorporate their best into your own design—which occupied you during Holy Mass, and on the ballfield, and mopping floors, let alone during classes of Sacred Dogma.

Every class period you drew in something new—node, calix, chasing—and took notes on *De Deo Creante et Elevante, De Deo Uno et Trino,* or *De Verbo Incarnato.*

Then you looked at what you had drawn, and erased it, only to draw it in better, as though you were working on the Holy Grail itself.

For precious stones I had searched through Sacred Scripture and found the description of the New Jerusalem—"And its foundations shall be of Jasper, and of Malachite, and Topaz." My father had a tie pin with a green stone in it which he wore in memory of Ireland; he said he would be delighted to donate it toward my chalice. I was beside myself when the jeweler identified it as chrysoprase, one of the very stones of the Bible.

But no one will understand—I do not understand it myself—what else I asked for. I asked my mother for her wedding ring.

It seems as though I almost stole it from them both. I felt that for my parents to be fused together through my chalice would be the greatest possible blessing.

You see, every chalice must have a cross at its base; some are magnificent. More than anything else, I wanted the ring to form a Celtic cross, with its circular halo of the sun, rising, the symbol of the Resurrection. "And ye shall have life," it would say, "forevermore."

I was thinking about the cross and putting one more curve on my chalice base when I heard Father Corkery's voice.

"Mister—what is Error?" Father Corkery was looking directly at me.

I sat upright, slid my notes forward almost into the back of Schunermann, and took a deep breath to recite the answer I carried well memorized within me.

"It means," I began, "that it is axiomatic that—"

Father Corkery would not let me continue. "Axiomatic!" he bellowed heavenward, his hands grasping the desk. "*Ax*—io—*mat*—ic?" He went on and on, shouting that this was not a course in Geometry, nor Arithmetic, nor Logic, no, nor mere Philosophy, even. It was a course in *Sacred and Dogmatic Theology*, in matters *De Fide Divina et Cattolica*, involving itself with the "Instruments of Revelation and the Magisterium of the Church" —not with "the theorems and axiomata of the *Unaided Intellect*," which, specifically in the tract under discussion, *De Novissimis*, addressed itself to the Four Last Things—a tract to which I would do well to attend.

He paused. I had never heard him speak so loud. I wondered if I was finished for good.

"Mister," he added, "it would appear that either you are doing too much reading in the wrong end of the library—" Mister Coon tittered expectantly—"or else you are seeing too much of your friends at Saint Elizabeth's!"

The class roared. Everyone knew that as my special apostolate I had chosen the work at "Saint E's," the huge Federal mental hospital in Washington's Southeast. The class dissolved with laughter at me. The great head turned elsewhere—to Mister Fred Barlow. I was free—bloodied, but still alive.

Mister Barlow was Father Corkery's secretary; we had lost time; we had had our laughter; Mister Barlow would get us back on the track.

Freddie recited. The Four Last Things were Death, Judgment, Heaven, and Hell. The Sacraments of the Dying included Holy Viaticum, from *"via"* and *"cum"*: to go on a journey with. What journey? The last, from which no traveler returns, death itself. Even the feet were anointed, in Extreme Unction. Why the feet? The feet of the Pilgrim, for it was a pilgrimage as well as a battle, the final one. The Cathari, the *Intransigenti*, this was their error, for in their invincible ignorance they rejected nothing less than the Church itself. What became of them? "They were burned alive, or hurled themselves off the cliffs of—of Mount—"

"Segur," I could hear Father Corkery saying, "Mount Segur, in southern France," and then there was silence.

I don't know what was wrong with me that morning; I could easily have avoided all that followed. But during Mr. Barlow's recitation I had stopped looking down at my notes and had raised my head; I was thinking and looking off, looking far off, into the vague space just above Father Corkery and beyond him, at the wall, really, when I saw that he was looking at me out of the corner of his eye. "Do you have a question?" he was asking.

In any words I spoke now, I knew, I would be fighting for life, for ordination. But I said them.

"Simon de Montfort and the Papacy of the time—were they not being un-Christian? I mean, to treat the mothers and the children like that? How do we square it with what Christ taught?"

Everything got very silent for a long time, as though Father Corkery were thinking. Then he said, in a soft tone, "It is a hard saying, Young Man, and who can hear it?"

He shook his head. "There were excesses—alas—on both sides. The history of this crusade—for though it was not exactly a pilgrimage to the Holy Land, that is what it was called—is harsh. On *both* sides, Gentlemen. Did you know that the heretics actually demanded the skull of Arnald, the Inquisitor, as a cup to drink from? The Holy

See *had* to act, had to hand over the *Innovatores* to what is called the Secular Arm—which did its business, that side of things not being the province of the Church."

He thought to himself for a moment. "The English poet John Milton—for, though English and Protestant, he was, Gentlemen, a fine poet—that man knew appallingly well what it means for the believer to be deprived of the Last Anointing. In 'Avenge O Lord Thy Slaughtered Saints'—do you know the poem?"

I shook my head; I had not read Milton.

"Whose bones lie scattered on the mountains cold,

he writes,

Mother with Infant rolled down the rocks!

And, lately, the American poet Robert Lowell—of more Catholic sensibility—applies it to the Protestants themselves:

Pilgrims unhouseled by Geneva's night . . .
And candles gutter by an empty altar.

'Unhouseled,' Gentlemen. 'Unanneled': *Unanointed*: the words are Shakespeare's! 'And candles gutter by an empty altar.'

"It is the Divine Magisterium of the Church you question, Mister! With the Modernists. NO!" He shook his head in rejection. "*Unam Sanctam! Unam Sanctam Ecclesiam!* One Church, there is but one Church, and it is the Catholic Church, and whoever would be saved must accept this, for outside that Church there is no salvation. *No salvation*, Gentlemen, the words mean what they say.

124

I do not care what Harvard says, I do not care what Anglicans say, I do not care what the Baptists say, or Luther, or Einstein: you cannot save yourself; no man is saved except through the Church! I don't care who they are—great intellects of this world or no—they find themselves with Dives the Rich Man, cut off eternally from their brother Lazarus, whom they thought to be poor, by a chasm which can never be bridged.

"A fierce, terrible doctrine which some would rather did not exist, but which is precisely the ancient doctrine of the Church in all eras of its history: he who will not heed is damned, and damned eternally.

"The Council of Florence: 'Whoever denies this, Let him be Anathema. 'A.S.,' Gentlemen, 'A.S.': *Anathema sit.* And Trent, 'Whoever asserts otherwise, *Anathema sit.*' And Vatican, 'Who would say the Pontiff is not infallible, *Anathema sit,* and *Vitandus sit'*: Let him be cut off. With Fire and Sword will He come to judge the living and the dead!"

He looked directly at me and said, "Sir. You are a Theologian. Charity does not rule Truth; it is the Truth which rules even Charity. And if Charity is not ruled by Truth, then it is Error and there is no room for it. There can be no room for a Charity informed by Error."

I knew everything he was talking about; I had heard it for four years, and found my lips enunciating each syllable with him, his phrases along with those I had memorized, ahead of him, more accurately at times, even outstripping him. *Anathema sit.*

I understood perfectly well the Church doctrine of nineteen centuries and I believed it as thoroughly as he did. The only question I had asked was "How?"

Father Corkery glanced up for a moment at the Great

Schema; generally at this point he would make one grand effort to reach the end. Instead, however, he pulled the cord and let the chart roll up and, looking directly at me, said, "Do you have any more questions?" I shook my head, No.

We had come to the end of the period. He was not satisfied. "Mister, I believe you are overdue for Monitions? Come up to my office at eleven on Friday."

Father Corkery began his usual sweep from the room; but as he mounted the curve of the amphitheater past my desk, he looked down and noticed the drawing of my chalice.

"Perhaps it is a bit premature for that," he said, and strode out of the Aula.

"Pee-yew! Peeeeee-yew! Pull that chain on that stuff, will you? Pull the chain! Someone in here must have swallowed a dead cat!"

It was the voice of Schunermann.

I had gone directly out of Dogma up to the fourth-floor jake; I wanted a moment of peace before next class—Advanced Pulpit Eloquence. I selected a booth, closed the door, threw my cassock skirt and cincture over my shoulder, lowered my pants, and sat down.

Then I heard Dick Schunermann coming down the hall; he was singing, and breaking silence.

"Oh, if you get there before I do," he was singing, off key, "just dig a hole and pull me through!"

He came into the booth next to mine, recognized my right shoe, and carried on about cats. "Pull the chain!" he kept saying. "Pull the chain on that stuff!" Then he laughed and laughed.

He farted loudly, groaned, and said, "Hey, why do you

wave a red flag at him like that? You're crazy! Say something, say anything! Just string him along with what he wants to hear and get out. I don't do so well myself sometimes, but at least *I'll* get *ordained!"*

Maybe so, I thought, without answering, to avoid breaking silence. I tried to think of something else, to preserve my private moment. Some of the men were impossible; in some ways we were just well-educated savages. Once, up in Michigan, in the town of Bessemer, our summer-camp bus stopped for lunch at noon. Mister Frank Roach, Schunermann's good friend, picked that moment to be sick; he put his head out of the window and was sick down the side of the bus.

Immediately, without any pause for sympathy, his good friend made up a song:

> "Old Frank Roach, he
> Yorked up in Bessemer,
> Yorked up in Bessemer,
> Yorked up in Bessemer,
> Old Frank Roach, he
> Yorked up in Bessemer . . ."

then, after a pause, added, "Many long years ago!" And with that, the rest of the bus, the whole house, picked it up and wouldn't let it stop, and Schunermann led us in the song, over and over, all the way to Tomahawk, Wisconsin. *Puer aeternus.*

One time we went by train, and Father Lucy for the sake of poverty made us eat our main meal out of a picnic box back in the coaches; then he sent us up, six by six in our black suits, to the diner car to have dessert: each man was to have coffee and pie. There was a huge black waiter there, enjoying his work, with a huge, happy smile.

He took our orders: six after six in clerical suits, all ordering the same thing. Finally he came to Mr. A. J. Bates, one of the two Canadians, and "A. J." also ordered "Apple pie and coffee." The huge black waiter's smile disappeared, he threw up his hands and in a loud voice shouted to the whole diner, "WHAT KIND OF RELIGION IS IT THAT DON'T ALLOW YOU TO EAT?"

My friendship with Schunermann started when he was in First Theology, in Moral class. First Moral meant many ethical principles to be memorized: *"Res Clamat ad dominum"* for example,—"the stolen thing cries out for its owner", and "in Confession the penitent is to be believed," and *"Nemo judex sui causa,"*—"No one is a good judge of his own case." That day, the day we met, the class was about the distinction between what was truly obscene, pornographic, or enticing to evil, and those things which were classed as frank, coarse, and "merely vulgar." The latter, though often impolite and offensive, could be classed as no more than a fault, not a sin. The ruddy naturalness of Geoffrey Chaucer, for instance, did not keep him from being profoundly Christian, and even Catholic.

Schunermann was delighted; he came to me at once after my second year class and announced that he had a joke to test me with, to see whether I understood the difference between what was evilly obscene and that which was merely vulgar: "There was this Britisher, see, sitting in a theater, who had a big bald dome on him. Right up above him in the gallery was a drunk. In the middle of the play, the drunk decided to have a pee, and just cut loose. The Britisher took it as long as he could, then he shouted up, 'I say there, Old Fellow! Couldn't you *bobble* it a bit? Yes I'm getting it *all*, you know!' "

I roared with laughter that first time, and for the next three years. Every morning during smoke period he would tell me another: Schunermann, cigar butt in the corner of his mouth jiggling in anticipation of the punch line, and badly needing a shave, Schunermann would be merely vulgar.

But my problem: I was in serious trouble. If I could not convince Father Corkery in Monitions that Friday of my sincerity and the genuineness of my Catholic Faith, I could forget forever my goal of the priesthood—something I honestly knew would make me consider suicide. And, to make it worse, my mother would be visiting me that weekend; I had asked her to come, to arrange final details for my First Mass.

It was Tuesday. I began to think of what to say to Father Corkery, and what he would ask about: Albigensianism, the Chapter of Trent and its Scholions, the teachings of the Church on the rights of Error, and anything else he might ask.

I had been there long enough. I pulled up my pants, dropped my cassock skirt and cincture into place, and started to head back to class.

"—Hey" came from the next booth with a snicker. "Before you go—pull the chain again, will you?"

I pulled the chain one more unnecessary time, and departed for Advanced Pulpit Eloquence, leaving Schunermann to his biological functions.

My strategy was to last out until Sacred Scripture at eleven, which was always like water in the desert. I looked forward to it every morning; it reminded me of that psalm we sang—*"Sicut Cervus desiderat ad Fontes Aquarum"*:

As the Hart seeketh and panteth
after the waterbrooks,
So does my Soul long and faint
for the Courts of the Lord!

That morning at eleven Father Jo Mac was in the Wilderness with David, being pursued by Saul, shouting back at him, "Why do you come out against me, as men hunt a partridge in the mountains?"

Jo Mac was saying in his quiet voice, "*Kings* is really the story of the Ark—the Ark of the Covenant, made from God's blueprints 'out of beaten gold and acacia wood, six cubits high,' to house the symbols of God's testament with Man, saying, 'This covenant shall not pass, it will not be broken . . .' and all that. And yet they lost it, lost it at once, brought down from Shiloh in the battle. And your book says, 'It has not been reported since the time of Nebuchadnezzar.' "

Jo Mac stopped and thought about how long ago that was.

I thought about things. About certain restful things, very often the *same* things; I continued to draw—not bombers, but more abstract little curlicues of design that let me think.

I thought most often of "the Question," of course. Each year, on the Feast of the Circumcision, January 1, a notice went up telling what "the Question" was which was to be defended at the end of the academic year in May at the Theological Disputation, along with the name of the Defensor Thesis. One man would be named to defend a thesis—usually one of the questions of the *Summa Theologica*. The Question for the previous year had been Whether God alone is Eternal, or not? And the year before it had dealt with the Moral principle *"Res clamat ad Dominum"*—"the stolen thing cries out after its true owner."

The Defensor graduated with his classmates at ordination, but the Question was fought tooth and nail by those left behind. That meant in summer camp at Shenandoah, on the border of Virginia and West Virginia, where to escape the heat of Washington we were able to pursue the tracts of the *Quadrivium* even in the months of June, July, and August.

The Shenandoah was Civil War country; all the time we were there, we never got very far away from the fact that it was still in the war's grip: incredibly old veterans who had been chore boys at Manassas and Richmond sat on the Post Office porch and told us how General Lee had been after the local freight yards on his way to Gettysburg, that Stonewall Jackson had had his headquarters at Winchester, that Antietam was only miles away. That first year, going in to get the mail for the first time, Joe Stroot had asked them how the weather was. Old Eli Browning, oldest of them all, said that it was all right, but that "It ain't bin what it's *bin* bin!" They told us other things as we got better acquainted—how Terra Alta, as Latin a name as ever came out of *Bennett's Latin Grammar*—was in fact something else: "Terry Alty? Why, that's an old Indian name," they assured us, and went on to tell us about Shiloh, and Bull Run, and The Wilderness. And from time to time one of us would ask if they could give us the old Rebel Yell.

We were not to call it "camp": it was the Summer House of Studies, and its formal name was The Villa of Our Lady of Lake Albano e Monte Cavo, a name which appeared in Latin over the fireplace upon the Sacred

Indult from the Sacred Congregation of Religion in Rome granting its foundation, a name selected by a past Superior out of a dreamy memory of his own happy days of summer study in the Alban hills of Rome, in the years before the war.

Camp meant work—we had the same Order of the Day —but it meant some release as well. A Navy lifeboat from war-surplus sales at Fort Myers was hauled out every evening after supper. The *Ark*, we called it. Nick Langendurfer would man the engine, Father Alcedo would bring some Frascati wine, perhaps, and Dick Gorman would lead us in song. Down past Old Baldy, under the huge bulk of Roman Nose Mountain, past Cherry Cove, to Echo Cove. On the way we would sing: "Swing Low, Sweet Chariot," "Mine Eyes Have Seen the Glory," "O Shenandoah," and Dick's favorite, "This Was a Real Nice Clambake."

Between songs we would argue; we would refight the Question; in Latin, English, and pig-Latin we shouted all that we had learned in class, and in our own delvings, and it got very heated.

That previous summer the camp had been host to a Protestant Minister and his young son—we were asked to be kind to them, for they were "Our Separated Brethren." The Minister was pleasant, but his child was atrocious. The boy had remarkable language. He had only two answers to any question; he said either "Hell No!" or, if he agreed, "Shit Yeah!" We began to try to get him to answer something else, until it became a game and the whole house broke out in the language: "Hell No!" and "Shit Yeah!" were heard everywhere. The boy became in the end unbearable—he poured a whole bottle of bleach into Moose Mulcahy's laundry bag, and Moose had to be restrained. But long after he left, his language remained.

One night that summer, afterward, when Langendurfer had stopped the engine at Echo Cove, Joe Stroot stood up in the boat: "Moose!" he shouted, and "Moose-oos-ooose" came back. Then he shouted, "Kick-ass!" and "ass-ass-ass" came back, followed by the echo of our laughter. Jimmy O'Shea pretended to go formal: *"Ho Men—Ho Day!"* he shouted, the Greek for the Question, Either/Or—*Utrum/An*. Everyone started showing off their knowledge, shouting learned scraps of the *Summa* at the West Virginia hillside. Finally Joe Stroot, who had started it, managed to get out the entire Question from that year's *Disputatio*, about the Eternality of God, ending with the *"An non?"* There was a pause, for the mountain could not answer that long a question, and someone shouted, "Hell No!" The mountain answered, "Hell No," then everyone said, "Shit Yeah," and, with no one else to hear, Echo Cove in western Maryland echoed, "Shit Yeah, Shit Yeah, Shit Yeah," and our laughter.

My mind struggled to return to Jo Mac's lecture; he was describing how Saul asked the Witch of Endor to call Samuel back from Sheol, the Abode of the Spirits. And the dead prophet came trailing the dust of the grave and his winding sheets behind him, approaching the terrified Saul with outstretched finger. "Why have you disturbed my rest?" he asked. "Why have you called my Spirit forth? For the Lord is departed from thee, and become thy enemy, and thy house shall fall, and you shall die, upon the side of Mount Gilboa, and remain among Israel no more."

I took notes dutifully, grateful for the respite. But the problems of Saul were his problems, not mine. I had my own: eleven years of effort—everything I was, really—hung by what would happen on Friday.

One thing I decided: I would not crack. I would keep myself busy. I would go to things, throw myself into the work at Saint Elizabeth's Hospital, attend Hearings at the Senate. I would think hard of what to say, but would not let it get to me. At noon I would sign up for a group going down to the National Gallery of Art, which we called "the Mellon." I would join them and go off looking at the pictures by myself, to find the peace I needed, to think and meet my problems.

The bell rang; we closed our books; David was telling Jonathan he had loved him more than a woman.

At the Mellon, with its maze of velvet-tasseled cords, Hermes, pagan messenger, greeted you on flying feet over the heads of tourists. I paused to feel the fountain's falling water rinse away the heat of Washington, and darted, alone, through the black columns. Then came statues of women, velvet cords channeling you on: "And here we see Ariadne," a voice said, "abandoned on Naxos, and there Europa with the Bull. . . ."

And I hurried past the Madonnas, and the Protestant altar triptychs—enough of that back at the college, without the Error. I stopped briefly when I came to Perugino and his angels. Vasari said that Perugino did not believe in the religion he painted; yet his angels made me pause for something that was in them. I glanced behind me for McInerny and Barlow, then I went on.

"Landscape painting came in through the window," someone had told me. "Look at medieval painting: it is all miracles, and saints, inside churches. But there is always a window, where the artist painted in the world: sky, mountains, trees, birds."

He was right, and it tickled me. The birds were mostly doves and crows, and at first they sat on branches. But as painting progressed and the modern world came on, the birds flitted from tree to tree, the trees became forests, and finally the sky and the earth took over the whole painting. I watched it happen.

But what I needed was farther on.

I could not say what it was. It had something to do with how Monet and Corot and the others caught the light of day coming down in one place, in one time. The place had a name such as Harfleur, or Pontoise, and the time seemed to be a very precise moment, say 1:53 in the afternoon, or 2:11.

But it wasn't the painting itself—though I loved the pigment and the gallery smells of canvas and linseed. It was that I was looking at what they saw on another afternoon: the world, or reality, or existence, or life itself— whatever name you gave it. I spent my afternoon at peace with what they saw. It was the thing I needed; it was, really, the closest I ever got to what the Holy Rule called "Meditation"; and it was one of those very few times I could say I was happy.

"Where *are* you! Where have you *been?* We're leaving now—we're going back to the House. You'll be late!" Freddie Barlow and Frank McInerny had come looking for me. I told them I would find my way home by myself.

I let some time go by, and went out into the street. There, on the corner of Constitution and Pennsylvania avenues, I saw Schunermann. He was smoking, right on

Pennsylvania Avenue. I went up to him and asked him why he was smoking in public, right on Pennsylvania Avenue. He didn't even remove the sloppy roll-your-own, fag-end that drooped from his mouth. "—Park," he said, pointing downward, "—Park." I looked down. We were standing on a triangular traffic island that could not have been thirty feet long; but it had bushes, and to Schunermann it was a "park" and he could smoke. He had his own way of spending his afternoons.

"You all right?" he asked me. "I saw you in there. You okay?" I assured him I was; anyone who looked at paintings was to Schunermann a little bit odd.

That quieted him, and after he finished his cigarette, we went back to the House together.

"We saw Senator McCarthy today," said Mister Blaes that evening at table. "He came over and talked to Rolly."

The irrepressible Rolly Hunter was a lovable Canadian who laughed so hard we sometimes thought he might die. He was in love with big trucks, their air-brakes; in the contemplative silence of the corridors—which Rolly never broke by speech—you were aware of his presence: "Chih!" you would hear behind you, "Chih!" and then "Chich-chich-chich!" It would be Rolly on his way to Church History or the refectory, air-braking to keep from running you down. Rolly, first one up the Washington Monument, first to walk to Andrews Air Base, first to hold a million dollars in his arms at the Government Printing Office, and, now, first to talk with Senator McCarthy.

"What did he say to you, Rolly?" I asked.

Rolly's face got red and he started giggling. "He said,

'Father—' he called me *Father*—'I hope you men are en-joying today's session.'

"I asked him what he thought about Senator Syming-ton, and he said that he would rather not say it in the presence of a priest!" Rolly's delighted face lit up with suppressed laughter. "But he called Senator Symington a *pismire!* A *pink* pismire!" Rolly laughed uncontrol-lably.

The men chatted on about the Senate Hearings, and certain names were mentioned: David Schine, Roy Cohn, Senator Mundt, Army Secretary Stevens, and as they talked I thought back: somehow, between Perugino's angels at the Mellon and Rolly's laughter, I had gotten through the day. I would have to think of some way to get me through to Friday—throw myself into the work at Saint Elizabeth's, study the twists and turns of the Great *Schema* of Denziger, and remain calm enough to talk with Father Corkery. Most of all, I would have to try to keep from worrying too much about my mother's visit.

"May the Lord look sideways at it—ah, sure, may the Good Lord look sideways at the poor little thing!" My mother is speaking. She is standing on a hillside, back in Pittsburgh, in that incredible turn-of-the-century hat she saved for sun and wind. Her wren, which returned year after year, has stolen yet another piece of brightly colored thread from the porch, and is fluttering bravely with it, up, up to its home in the poplars. It is her favorite prayer: that God will not see, will pretend not to see the small knaveries of his universe: May the Lord look sideways.

She seemed to attract the blue sky, with birds in it. Whenever I feared she was gone, had left us for good, like all the songs said, I would go running out, to find her at peace, in her field, among the poppies and the wild flowers. I would run beyond her down over the slope, rousing grasshoppers. As my head bobbed up and down among the wild rose and berry vines, I would look up every so often, to everything I loved: the sky and the birds and the orchard and the old house and the songbird and my mother, still there and not gone away at all.

It is a moment I would have an artist paint. Put in vineyards, I would tell the artist, and let there be an orchard. Make her beautiful, *much* more beautiful—let there be, on that starving Pittsburgh hillside, still something of the Hebrides, of cold Northern Ireland, and have her thinking of something. Make the moment last, if you can. . . . Do not have the house too freshly painted, and have her with her back to it, as though she is not *entirely* pleased with what it gave her. And oh—could you include the old turn-of-the-century hat, without making her in any way ridiculous—a hand raised to its brim, like those ladies in the Mellon?

I despair of ever finding such a painter.

My Father had a saying: "After the Fourth of July, sure, the summer's back is broken!" which we nodded to, and waited for the first locust. Other people call them cicadas, but in Pittsburgh they are locusts, and once their first long-drawn, melancholy sound is heard, high in the summer poplars, you know that the dog days are upon you, and that autumn must not be far behind.

It affected me deeply, that saying, for I wanted the summer to be one long, endless Fourth of July, with sky-rockets and Roman Candles and sparklers going off eternally, and no school to be feared, no September round the corner. But as it went on, with summer's back broken and the locusts saying something to me over and over from high in the lovely poplars, I ran and ran, in Hide and Seek, and Run Sheepy Run and Kick the Can, and rushed into the house to get cold water from the faucet so that I might run out and run some more, but in short, I was afraid.

She did the best she could for me, for she wanted more than anything else on earth to see me safely in the arms of Jesus and His Blessed Mother Mary eternally, and though she scrupulously respected my freedom of choice, still, like a mother hen with her chick, she fostered me toward it from an early age, toward the best thing there was, the best thing by far there was in this whole created universe—the ordination to the priesthood of the Roman Catholic Church. And in the end I wanted it more, and for deeper reasons, than she could know, more than anything else on earth, for the reasons that Augustine of Carthage gave, and the Martyr Thomas à Becket gave, and, of course, for the reasons given by that Doctor of the Church, the incomparable John of the Cross himself.

That evening, going up to my cell to study Dogma, I could not concentrate for fear of Corkery: he would destroy me on Friday, for I was not up to disputing with him yet. Or I would destroy myself: some questions really did give me pause; my mind was not totally at peace with it all. And as I tried to force it to think, my mind kept going back to other things.

As children we had a game we played. Whenever you found a "thistle"—the silvery seed of the plant wafting along through the air—you captured it and made a wish, for whatever wish you made upon a thistle would surely come true. I never told my wish to the others, it was too private. They wished for motorcycles or ponies or a box seat behind the Pittsburgh Pirate dugout. I closed my eyes over my clasped hands and wished very hard that my father would be King and my mother would be Queen; that took care of me, too—then I opened my palms to see if it was still there, and blew upward. The thistle shot upward, and I went blowing after it, until finally the wind would catch it and take it up, high over Connollys', over their roof and past their chimney, into the poplars and it was gone.

The Retirement bell rang; I had not done my tract, and had not even prepared well for the next day's work at Saint Elizabeth's. May the Lord look sideways. I made another resolution not to let my mind wander; I would throw myself into the work at Saint E's—that would leave only one more day to Friday. I turned in.

My job at Howard Hall Maximum Security Facility for the Criminally Insane was to conduct choir practice on Wednesdays for Mass on Sundays, and for the Miraculous Medal Novena which followed it. The Miraculous Medal Novena of Saint Catherine Labouré had miraculous properties, even beyond those of the rosary itself. Nothing was too much to ask for: cure from mental illness, release from imprisonment, return to one's family, and, of course, avoidance of the horrid operation called Prefrontal Lobotomy, for in the Saint Elizabeth's Hospital of Doctor Winifred Overholzer the solution to the condition of being "criminally insane" was often this operation: the surgical separating of the front lobes of the brain from the rear lobes.

I would make my arm a metronome as we prayed our
song:

> "Mother Dearest, Mother Fairest,
> Help of all who call on Thee,
> Mother Sweetest, Brightest, Rarest,

> "Mary, help us, help we pray!
> Mary, help us! Help we pray!"

After the hymn I would pass out strings of rosary beads
to the men who would crowd up, or Miraculous Medals.
Howard Hall frightened me, more than even the wards
like MR, Men's Receiving, or WR, Women's Receiving.
In those buildings I had trouble keeping the Male and
Female keys separate and not getting locked in with
patients, especially in stripped cells, which did happen
to me a few times. Howard Hall was different, starting
with the armor-plate door off the old battleship *Utah*,
down through the stairway leading into "hell" and the
little alcoholic Charon at the entrance, then up into the
various levels full of steel staircases and wire mesh. I did
get used to it, for each week I saw the same things: one
patient, totally naked except for a steel-cupped athletic
supporter (either for his safety or someone else's, I never
knew for sure); another tall man, standing rigidly in one
position ("catatonic," his file said, back at the Registrar's
Office); and a man who added up endless columns of
numbers on toilet paper, an accountant said to have been
implicated in the Teapot Dome scandal, still adding
figures decades later, still trying to make them come out
right. He did them all through Mass, and through the
sermon, and handed them to you at the door—sometimes
he put them in the collection basket. There was Antonel-

li, and Stacey, and there was Clyde Stickles, due for his brain operation, who always wanted another rosary.

There was also one George Gundell, a retarded boy in his teens who had not done anything criminal, but who was such a burly elephant of a boy that even Howard Hall couldn't contain him. He wore a hearing aid, and was always walking up to the attendant's station asking for batteries. If the door was closed, or if the attendant refused, Gundell would kick and slam the door with frightening violence.

"Why did God make you, Gundell?" I asked, for it was my job to take him through his Catechism.

Gundell looked out the window at a gravel truck. "Wave," he said. "Wave!" That meant "gravel," I knew—we had been through it before.

"Yes, Gundell, grav-el. And why did God make you?"

Gundell walked over to the attendant, slammed into the door a few times, and came back with more batteries. I was on the next page, the Incarnation, and was starting to say the name "Jesus" for him clearly, when suddenly Gundell started shouting, "Shoo! Shoo!" at me, the lesson was clearly over, and we were moving to the door. Gundell was shouting at the top of his lungs. But he wasn't coming after me, and he didn't want me to leave. So I did what I always did: I reached in my pocket and pulled out a string of rosary beads.

"Shoo!" said Gundell. "Shoo!" He grasped the crucifix at the end of the beads and said, "Shoo" and kissed Jesus over and over. "Shoo" was Jesus, as well as he could say it.

I nodded, and said, "*Yes*, George—*Yea*-shoo, *Yea*-shoo . . ."

The lesson was over, and after I went through the door I wondered if I should say one more "Jesus," but Gundell was already at the equipment cabinet, pounding on it for new batteries. The little man inside was very firm, he said no more batteries, use the ones you already have, and George turned to his comic book.

We did try to sing liturgical songs at certain times, and on Ash Wednesday of my first year at Saint Elizabeth's a strange man, stranger than the others even, with a pointed beard and piercing eyes, spoke up. "Brother!" he shouted at me. "Brother! When do we get to Josquin? When is the Josquin?"

I knew at once who it was; I knew from the question. It was Mister Ezra Pound, for I had been told about him. He was not in Howard Hall at that time, he was in Chestnut, but that year he must have gotten himself sent over for the music. He was referring to Josquin des Prés, the great medieval composer, and wanted to sing the *"O Vos Omnes."*

I looked around at my choir; all they really knew was "Mother Dearest." I decided to chance it; we turned to page 1787 in the *Liber Usualis*, and found *"O Vos Omnes."*

It was hopeless; the men didn't know it, and Pound kept singing it out with a stupendous Italian accent, like an opera star. They kept looking around at him, and everything fell to pieces, and finally I stopped and in a loud voice said, *"Extra choram cantat!"* Pound roared with laughter, delighted at the comment, and our friendship began.

The next Wednesday when I came in for practice, he shouted, "Brother, have you seen Whitman yet?"

First I thought he meant one of the patients; I said, "Do you mean Stacey or Campanella? They aren't here any more, they've gone up for their lobotomies."

"Nawwwwww," he said, "I mean American Walt! The old Grass Man, of Gold Durn and tell youse all. I have to show him to you—Paumanok and all that. You *need* him, Brother!"

I looked at him guardedly; I was not interested in poetry, but Mister Pound kept taking it that I was. It had actually been my policy to avoid the famous man, for I strongly felt I was there for other reasons. I did succeed in avoiding him until after Holy Week that year, but when I finally showed up at Chestnut, I saw Ezra Pound waving a book at me and saying, "Paumanok!" It was, I now comprehend, a volume containing "Out of the Cradle Endlessly Rocking."

He sat me down on the porch and read it out to the lawn in a loud voice. Other patients gathered around and looked; I felt embarrassed in my black suit.

"Land! Land! Land!" he cried, and "Shine! Shine! Shine!" and it was all about lilacs and ocean waves and a poor bird singing, all about a child getting up at night to go down to the Long Island shore to listen to the singing of a sea bird that had lost his mate, but would not go away, calling out endlessly to her to return. I knew from the way he read it that the boy standing on the shore was Whitman himself, and "the savage old mother" was the undertow of the ocean, whispering one word to the boy over and over, which the poem itself would not utter. And when he finally finished it, with the lines,

> A word then, (for I will conquer it,)
> The word final, superior to all,
> Subtle, sent up—what is it?—I listen:
> Are you whispering it, and have been
> all the time, you sea waves?

I fairly jumped in my shoes to say what I thought. He ended, and I said, "But it's about *death*. The poem is about dying!" Pound doubled up as though he had done something mischievous. "So's Homer!" he said. "So's Dante! So's Shakespeare!" and he laughed some more.

I went off shaking my head at such a ridiculous teacher. I never knew who I passed in the people waiting to see him, though I know, of course, that T. S. Eliot, Robert Frost, and many others frequented that hallway.

Why was I spending so much time with Ezra Pound? Why was I talking about things I knew nothing of? That was easy. Though no one ever bothered to ask the question, I and any of my fellow seminarians could have answered at once: I was there to convert him to Catholicism—I was there to save the soul of Ezra Pound.

He continued my education for the rest of that first year, and on up through all four years. I would leave Howard Hall, and each week as I headed toward Chestnut it was the same: I would run into "General Custer," a harmless patient in a frontiersman outfit, complete with rawhide and stunning cowboy hat, whose duty it was to thread his way around each of the hospital's ninety buildings and touch each building twice each day. He was always in a hurry, but touched his brim smartly as we passed. I always knew where I was when I heard a lady's voice coming down from one of the higher women's wards calling names at me: "Cock-roach! Cock-roach! Here comes the Cock-roach!" and there would be laughter, and then she would say, "Beetle! Black Beetle! Look at the black Beetle!" and laugh some more. She called me cockroach and beetle for four years. I would stop next and see my Indian friends Dorothy Fasthorse and May Goodshield, for the hospital was Federal and served the

Indian Reservations. And then I would stop to visit Mister Pound. His wife, Dorothy, often gave me cookies.

And so each time, after I had finished choir practice, I would head over to Chestnut for what turned out to be a poetry lesson.

He thought it a crime for a cleric not to know the poets Richard Crashaw and Henry Vaughan, and waved a different book at me each time. "Holy Mister Herbert!" he would shout from the veranda. "The metaphysicals!"

" 'I saw Eternity the other night!' " he bellowed, clenching his fists, and then

"They are all gone into the world of light!"

finishing quietly with

"And I alone sit lingering here. . . ."

It was mainly to get me to Walt Whitman, however; he thought that the American poet would save my soul. One Wednesday I realized something; and at the end of our session I spoke about it bravely, not caring how he took it. I said, "Oh, Mister Pound, I see what has happened—we have stopped worrying about *your* soul, and are worrying about *mine!*"

He laughed harder than I had ever heard him, and I could still hear him roaring as I passed P Building; but when I looked down, I saw a copy of *Sweet's Anglo-Saxon Reader* had been tucked into my coat pocket.

And after Whitman it was John Donne. I can still hear his voice reciting it out toward Nichols Avenue: Donne going to confession to the Father in Heaven:

I have a sin of fear, that when I have spun
My last thread, I shall perish on the shore;
Swear by Thy self, that at my death Thy Son

Shall shine as he shines now and heretofore;
And, having done that, Thou hast done,
I fear no more.

I halted him, and asked, "Why the thread? Does he think he's a spider? You know what I think? I think it's this Naxos thing you're always talking about. After Ariadne spun her thread for Theseus, he left her naked upon the shore, then God abandoned her. *Maybe it's like Christianity:* God is always the Bridegroom, and the Soul is his Bride. Donne is thinking of himself as Ariadne abandoned on the beach; he's using the Greek myth for Christian purposes."

When I said this, I was very self-conscious and I had spoken in a mock-serious tone, to forestall criticism. Pound came up to me and hit me a wallop between the shoulderblades. "You serious about this priesthood thing? You still serious?"

At least he had listened. He was a difficult teacher.

But if the truth were known, by that particular Wednesday in the spring of what I hoped would be my ordination, I was beginning to feel that I had perhaps had enough of Mister Ezra Pound. I had given up trying to convert him to Catholicism—that was even more ridiculous than trying to direct him in choir. One way or another, I would be leaving shortly, and did not know what I could possibly ever do with the things he taught me.

That afternoon Mister Pound was finishing a visit by a distinguished-looking gentleman, and his wife, Dorothy, was there. He shouted at me, "How's the *calix* coming? The smaragdus, the chrysoprase?" I replied that it was in the hands of Domgoldschmiedehaus now, except for one item, and that I had other things to think about, notably the tract *De Novissimis*; I would have an examination on the Sacrament of Extreme Unction in the private quarters of Father Corkery that Friday, and if I didn't pass that, my chalice—and a lot of other things—would become a piece of lunacy.

"*Unam Sanctam!*" he roared. "*Istam Sanctam unctionem!*" and he went roaring on about the Albigenses and the ruins on their mountaintop and "the *bonhommes*"—the "good men"—and how nothing now was left but the sun and the wind and the rain.

It wasn't helping me; he reminded me of my father carrying on about Roosevelt; I still had to get through Friday. Pound lost his temper, trying to make me see, until Dorothy said, "Ezra, let the young man make up his own mind."

He had gone over to a window, looking out through the heavy wire-screen mesh, and when he came back he was calm. He sat down opposite me and looked straight into my eyes. "Brother," he said, "it doesn't matter whether you're in the Cork's place or Doctor Winifred Overholzer's St. E's, they both separate the soul from the body. Doctor does it with preeeeee—front—alll lo—bot—o—my; Cork does it more slowly, over the years. *Arbor Vitae*—Labyrinth of the Brain! You're ascairt of him, ain't you?"

I did not answer, except with my face, and that said, Anyone in my situation would be foolish not to be afraid of him.

"Well, that's an error," Pound replied. "Just how many young men has the Cork *devoured* all these years? Year after year, huh, year after year? We gotta get you outta the Cork's establishment! We gotta find some Ariadne to drop us a line! I might hafta rescue you myself!" Then he stopped a moment and laughed: "Of course, I could use a little thread too!" and he roared some more.

"Let the young man make up his own mind, Ezra," Dorothy said, handing us tea and some cookies she had made.

I felt better; and as I left to go back to the House of Theology to face my problems, I turned to Ezra Pound and whispered quietly, *"Pax tecum."*

He put his arm on my shoulder at the door and replied, *"Et cum spiritu tuo."*

Thursday was work day. Up at five, Mass at six; wait on table for breakfast; your own obedience, the stairways, then outdoor work. There was not time to think of anything. That spring we were putting in drainage pipes in the field behind the college, and I was detailed to it. It meant going down into the ditch fifteen feet deep in some places, and it was dangerous, and terribly hot down there in the Washington heat. Then to showers, and Chant Practice at four.

Father Hager took us through our "vocal eases" for pitch and timbre, "ha-hey-he-ho" all over the scale and back; then four perfect-pitch notes, syllables pronounced exaggeratedly for perfection: "Heennnnnng—Hayngggg —Hanggggg—Hungggggg" and we were ready. Ready for what? For Vittoria, or de Lassus, or Pergolesi: *"Christus factus est,"* or *"Vox clamantis,"* or *"Cantate Domino"*— notes quietly given to a superb choir about to sing the great music of civilization. After all these years they are the only thing I miss.

After choir, recitation of the Breviary, in private—there was really no time for me to worry, and I slept well that night.

I was strangely quiet, at peace, the morning of my Monitions. It was again the time of the seventeen-year locusts, and Washington drowsed to their soft, endless murmur. Brother Job and Brother Jonah were brightening up the recreation room, putting in splendid black and white tiles from Italy. It was the same classic design from ancient Crete which ran through the entire house, and when they finished, it would run, unbroken, from the High Altar in Chapel all the way down around our pool tables in the basement. During midmorning break I watched them, one preparing a piece of tile, then handing it to the other, who put it carefully in place to make a border. I sipped a cup of strong tea, and each time I raised the cup to my lips I looked to see what progress was being made. It seemed like something out of Corot, a moment in the morning mist, the sun not yet arrived, the Brothers happy to be doing something for young men so close to priesthood and their First Mass. I was wishing the moment would last forever, like the paintings in the Mellon, when Mister Klingenschmidt came up to me. "Father Corkery will see you now," he said.

I went to the kitchen, where Sister Bo Peep handed me out his tray, then I ran with it up the spiral stair.

It was custom, because of his arthritis, for a theologian to bring Father Corkery's meal up to his room every morning. First you got your tray at the window from one of the cloistered nuns, Sister Yogi Berra or Sister Bo Peep—we had nicknames for all of them—then found your way to the faculty wing. Father Corkery's suite was at the very end, and he himself was always in the inmost of the three rooms. The trip was frankly dangerous, for it was dark, and you had to wind your way past huge tomes and footstools. I got so that I turned when I saw certain titles gleaming: Lietzmann: *Catenen, 1897*; Mercati, *Variazione Catene del Psalterio. John Climacus.* Then I knew where I was when I came to the wall, the complete Ming's *Ante- and Post-Nicene Fathers*—a collection of inestimable value—and as I made my final turn, he would be sitting there, sitting on a huge oak *sedilia*, one leg raised on another footstool, reading *Time* magazine, or *Osservatore Romano.*

As soon as I set the tray down, Father Corkery began animated conversation. "And did you catch Sheen the other night (Where's the butter? Did Bo Peep forget the meat?)—talking about 'His Ball'? 'The Divine Child has lost His *ball*, Comrades! Let us get Him back His Ball!' Did you ever hear such tripe? *I thought he was going to say something else!*" Father Corkery let himself enjoy a tremendous bull-like snort. "The man's senile! Spellman should have him silenced! Ah, *prosciutto e melone!*"

Father Corkery plunged in. "You know he doesn't get along with Spellman?" I shook my head; I knew nothing. "Sheen raises the money for the *Propaganda Fidei*, of course, and he sends all those American dollars directly to the *Propaganda*, and the Italian Cardinals just think he's wonderful. It drives Spelly nuts. . . .

"And did you ever hear how Spellman got to be Cardinal?"

No.

"We were Romans together at the Gregorian University (Does she call this *stracciatelle?* The French can't make it)—at the Greg, and on the way over, on the old *Conte di Savoia*, Spelly had a little camera, one of the early Brownie Kodaks, and he took our pictures. But at the Greg you should have seen him operate that camera! Spelly got to know one of the Italian seminarians very well, by the name Eu—*gen*—eeee—o Pa—*celllll*—i! Every visiting day the entire Pacelli clan would come, you know how the Italians are, and Spellman would spend the day taking pictures. He was invited out to Orvieto, to Tivoli, and the Castelli Romani. After the war—well, you know the rest.

"So much for Papal Infallibility!" snorted Father Corkery. "Our class does have one other prelate—the Bishop of West Bend, Oregon! He's an alcoholic!"

Father Corkery turned the tray around and discovered the meat plate, which Bo Peep had not forgotten after all.

Silence. Nothing from me; I felt ignorant.

Suddenly Father Corkery looked straight at me and we were back in the Aula. "You have a look on your face sometimes in class as though you are not accepting all that is being presented. You appear to harbor doubts . . .

"Mister, I do not know what kind of half-savage monster you men take me to be, but I assure you I have my human side. I must warn you, however, that I am not without influence here; the House Council will not pass upon you for ordination without my approval; you will never get out of this House, ordained, you cannot escape my scrutiny. You are not unintelligent. Therefore, I repeat: Do you believe what is being taught in Sacred and Dogmatic Theology, or do you not? It is as simple as that. If I am in Error, please correct me. . . . I hope my ignorance will not prove invincible!

"Moreover, I have noticed you *drawing* in class. . . . I wish you would explain the need for that."

All the men drew; you could not sit through the four years of Moral, Scripture, Canon Law, Dogma, Liturgy, and Church History without resorting to it. I knew I was the worst, however, for in addition to the elaborate sketches of my chalice in its variations, the margins of my notes were illuminated and embroidered by an endless string of fighter planes, accurate down to every detail of auxiliary fuel tanks and "external stores": I knew well what I was drawing. I was grateful that Father Corkery had not mentioned the fighter planes.

"The reason I draw chalices—" I began. "I have been drawing them from the Sixth Grade, Father. That year we had an Art class for the first time. Sister Imelda had permission from the Pastor to get us an art book called *The House of God*, with colored pictures of the rose window from Chartres, and one of the Chalice of Rheims. I never saw anything so beautiful. I did a drawing of it, which Sister praised and hung up over the blackboard to show the class. That was the year I decided to become a priest—I was eleven—and I have been designing what I hope will be my own chalice ever since."

I looked at him, wondering if I should say more than that, but he was struggling with his plate and was distracted. He looked up at me briefly and smiled. "*All* the men talk about their chalices. . . ."

It was a blow; I had thought that even a few words on that subject would convey something of how I felt about the priesthood, that they would of course be overwhelmingly convincing, and we would not have to talk about that ever again, we could go on to the tract *De Novissimis* and the Albigensian Heresy like two theologians. But I realized: he sits here, and every day a different young man brings him a tray, and tells him about a different chalice.

"Can't you be . . . more *subs*tantive?" He was looking for silverware he had lost.

I was embarrassed by the way things were going, and my face burned, and I heard myself speak out in a loud voice of something I had never intended to speak of. "As for the authenticity of my attraction to the priesthood, I have often been concerned about that, too. I think that it is probably good for a person to check himself. Perhaps the best way to convince you is to tell you . . . well, to tell you what I tell myself. It is something that happened last summer at camp, at the Villa. We were on a truck picnic down to Black Water Falls. As you know, the current can be swift there. I unwisely decided to swim across the pool below the falls. I made it across all right, but when I got to the opposite shore, I found the rocks all sloping against me. I could not climb up. I had no strength to go back. I had difficulty breathing, and started to choke. I was, quite clearly, drowning. And the thought, the only thing that passed through my mind was the words 'as a seminarian—as a seminarian—as a seminarian—' It was inconceivable that God had brought me so far to abandon me there, without reaching the priesthood even to say one single Mass."

"And that was your last thought as you were going under—that you would die before being ordained? How did you get out?"

"I called, 'God . . . God . . .' Hank Hughes heard me and pulled me out. He was painting scenery there on the shore."

Father Corkery tossed his head back in disbelief. "Hank *Hughes?* Harold? You called to God and got Hank? Why, Jonas himself would have gone straight to the bottom! Lord save us. . . ."

Father Corkery with an eloquent Roman gesture indicated that his tolerance was at an end. He looked straight at me and said, "Mister, *you do not have a Vocation to the priesthood!* That is why I called you up here—to recommend that you stop considering that you have."

He busied himself about the tray, arranging for its return, searching for crumbs, pressing his napkin, letting me think.

"No," he said firmly, "you do not have a Vocation. You will not be called to priesthood until on ordination morning—if you reach it—over in the National Shrine when the ordaining Bishop (It's John Sheehan, isn't it?) calls out your name, you answer *'Adsum'* and take the step forward to the laying on of hands. At that moment, *then* you will have been called. All this . . . chalice . . . drowning—take it up with your Spiritual Director, it does not concern me. I am not allowed to deal with it in the External Forum, it is what we call Piety—Personal Piety, eh?" He looked at me as though we should be one Roman to another, as though we *knew* all these things and it was my sorry failure they had to be brought up at all.

"No! I am Chair of Sacred Dogma here. My interrogation can consist of only one thing. I am to ascertain whether you do accept the Divine Teaching Magisterium of the Church *totaliter*, completely, in all its entirety, or do you not? Either/Or—*Utrum/An?* Can you say, in the face of those things which seem impossible, what the

Roman centurian said: 'I do believe—Lord, help my un-
belief'? Or even what the Great Anselm said, at the utter
impossibility of the Trinity: '*Credo* quia *absurdum est*'?
—'I believe because it is absurd'? Satisfy me on that, and
you will be ordained.

"Two things you will have to do before I am satisfied.
One. It is very simple, but I am determined that you do
it. You will stop seeing Mister Ezra Pound. You are no
match for the kind of knowledge he has; and, for all his
faults, no one denies he is one of the geniuses of our time.
You are simply to stop seeing him." Father Corkery hardly bothered to check my response; the statement would
be sufficient.

"The second entails more difficulty. Mister Blaes has
become ill; he was to do the May *Disputatio*. The question is, as you know, '*Utrum extra ecclesia nulla salus,
An non?*' It is Father Feeney's fight with Harvard University, 'Outside the Church there is no salvation.' You
will be Defensor. You will defend that thesis, which is
nothing but straight Catholic doctrine; it should provide
the House Council with more than enough to pass judgment."

"I have done!" he said suddenly, looking down at the
empty tray. "*Causa finita est!*" I nodded and picked the
tray up, and as I started out of the room, he said, "Now,
off to your mother! She's a fine, Catholic woman!"

I found my way out, past Ming's *Fathers*, past the
Variazione and all the *Catenae*. I had not escaped. Everything instead had become even more tangled, if that was
possible, and now my mother was coming, too. What a
mess.

As I headed down the hall toward the kitchen, Mister

Schunermann just happened to be emerging from the stairway; he had been waiting. He approached me, looking straight ahead, solemnly keeping silence; he glanced at me as we passed; then he held his nose with one hand, and with the other began pulling vigorously on an imaginary chain. He knew that I was all right.

Bo Peep greeted me as I handed in my tray. "Mistaire," she said, "You 'ave return?"

"Yes, Sister," I said, "he killed it off. Father Corkery told me to tell you that he will take the *Sister* Novices next week. You're *next*." The kitchen window closed firmly in my face, and I went off to recreation.

My mother's visit was not a happy one like the first, when she had come down during the Truman Administration: that time the B&O conductor had asked her her destination and she said in a loud voice, "*Washington—* I'm going to get one of those mink coats!" and the entire car full of men roared in delight with the plucky old woman.

I had hoped to have good news; instead I spent the entire time making plans for a First Mass which might never come off, which were tentative, though I could not bring myself to tell her so. I took her to Mount Vernon, where she was at home—back in the Big House, back with the silver plate of the Presentation Convent, back with the Mellon family, whose children she had raised.

Saturday night we went to Olmstead's Restaurant on G Street, for the high point of the visit.

She had brought a parcel, something wrapped in tissue paper. At the end of the meal she brought it out: "I've brought you something; you forget, but you asked me for it a long time ago." She pulled back the layers of tissue and held up two strips of white linen, embroidered so that even in the dark of the restaurant you could see and feel that my mother had woven the ancient Celtic design of the infinite string or cord, doubling upon itself and intertwining with itself, having no breaks or false starts, something older than Patrick even, a string of something going back to the beginning, to whatever was there.

"The *panniculi* for the hands," I said, "for the anointing! The *panniculi*! I will give them to Brother Sacristan to keep until ordination morning."

That night in Olmstead's was like the last night of our lives somehow—as though things would move on and we would never talk again. She told me something. She said, "If you ever go to Galway—I am sure you will—ask to be shown 'The Silver Strand.' It is all changed now, but there when I was a girl it was my favorite place. It was all lonely, and I went down to it at night. The sand made it shine, and the sparkle of the periwinkles in the brine. There was a song we children sang—and we danced to it." And she told me of it: how the girls would sing a verse about things of long gone by, how they were there for a while but are gone—how nothing is left. It was in Irish, and she showed me there in the corner of the restaurant how the girls pirouetted.

I only remember parts of it, but I remember those clearly, for she repeated the Irish for it, and each refrain ended with the rending cry, "O Lord, let something remain!" It is the way I remember her, singing that: "O Lord, let something remain."

But there was something else in the package, something I had not forgotten and was waiting for; she had not forgotten either. She pointed to a little package in the white tissue around the *panniculi:* "My wedding ring," she said, "for the chalice . . . ." The waiter came; I paid the bill.

"Your chalice costs a lot," she said without stopping. "It is just barely what your father and I can afford. . . . This will help, though; it is what you asked for." And she uncovered the green chrysoprase from him.

Res clamat, I thought, but I said nothing; I could think of nothing; I nodded gratefully, embarrassed at their generosity; as we got up to leave, I folded the two items carefully into my suit pocket; I would airmail them to Trier in the morning; it was all Domgoldschmiedehaus was waiting for; I would have my chalice in two weeks.

Next morning, looking for relief from the *Disputatio*, I dropped in on Scripture class, which I was no longer required to attend. Father Jo Mac had gotten going on encyclopedias and scriptural dictionaries. "That one's up to the letter J," he was saying as I came in. "Knaben-bauer is working on it." He named another and said, "It's up to P—be done in this century or so. . . ."

But Bill Slaney, new from Minnesota, pen poised for a short, memorizable answer, asked in his booming voice if the passage the class was halted at did not in fact contain a clear reference to the Resurrection, and thus imply belief in eternal life?

I was delighted; I sat down. Jo Mac was about to give one of his celebrated non-answers. It was the wrong question, you see; after four years of Jo Mac, you knew that *any* question about the passage under analysis was the wrong question. Whatever you asked—and Jo Mac was surprised that you did not know—was always dealt with in quite another place, quite other passages entirely, no connection whatever, so that you wondered how he managed any religious faith himself, or if, indeed, he had any.

Jo Mac looked to the blank wall on the other side of the room; he looked as though he didn't know where the question came from, didn't know whether it *was* a question, wasn't concerned that it had an answer, and you could see him deciding to shock the young man, to throw cold water over the young man from Minnesota.

"—Resurrection?—" he said. "—Eternal life?—That's not in Scripture, not in the Bible. That's an Egyptian idea—that's what that old Sphinx is waiting for, out there in the corridor, old Mereneptah. . . . It's not in the Old Testament—unless you adduce Maccabees—you're not going to adduce Maccabees, are you?"

Slaney crumpled; you could almost read his lips saying, If Sacred Scripture is not about this, what is it about? (I knew that look, I had had it on my face, too.) But Jo Mac had decided to go on about Mereneptah.

"No—no—no—if you're going to look for that, you'll have to look someplace else—the other Testament."

Jo Mac thought awhile; Slaney, forgotten, was looking through his book for something to take notes on.

"They saw the Nile, they saw life rising again, each season, out of the Nile mud, you see, and appointed a god for it, in charge of Resurrection—the different ones, Isis, Osiris, and Ptah, the Creator God. That's who—your Sphinx is out there, Mereneptah—The One Beloved of Ptah, which is to say, the One Who Will Rise Again. Except, do you know the story? It's not *him*, it's not even *him*; that statue is of someone else entirely!

"You know the story? You see, Rameses, Pharaoh of the Oppression, was the greatest builder of all time. And he put the seal of resurrection on everything—his own seal, his cartouche, a coil of rope. That divine cord tied in a magic circle bound up all that was mortal of him, on ship for eternity: 'It is Rameses,' the inscription said, 'who will live forever!'

"But Mereneptah, puny successor, one of thirteen sons, Pharaoh of the Exodus, had his royal chiselers in—" we laughed at the "royal chiselers"—"had them chisel off the old cartouche—you can still see where they did it, run your hand along the basalt on the shoulder of the lion—had them break the cord, scrubble off the coil that bound in his mighty predecessor, and replace it with his own *sigillum* of a lie, and made it say, 'This is Mereneptah: it is Mereneptah who will live forever!'"

Jo Mac was telling us the story he told roughly four times a semester; I was hearing it, therefore, possibly for the thirty-second time. He was telling us that we had Mereneptah—Pharaoh of Aaron's Rod, the Plagues, the Passover Pharaoh, of the Red Sea and the Wanderings—right there in the House with us.

"No one was fooled. Oh, maybe Anubis, the Jackal God, or Horus of the Horizon—perhaps—foolish things, *they* were. . . .

"But the grave-robbers were not. It came out with all the booty. Father Merganthaler found it on the docks at Alexandria and shipped it here, thinking of you people. He was a friend of Teddy Roosevelt, you know."

Slaney was writing notes; undoubtedly they were

about the text the class was supposed to be discussing. *Someone* had to act responsibly.

Jo Mac was working his way back to the letter P again, and I slipped out, amused by how predictable it had all been.

Something shocking happened on the eve of the *Disputatio*. Rolly Hunter asked my help in filling out a request for Dispensation from his vows. That meant Rolly was leaving, or trying to leave, before ordination. I gasped, I hated to think of Rolly going, and I could not think of Rolly separate from A.J. or the rest of us.

He wanted to do it right; there were 132 questions on the form; he wanted me to read each question out aloud—he had been through it many times—so that he could double-check his answers, to be sure that he was answering right.

I had never seen a Dispensation before, but it was about what I expected: it was all *"Ad Mentem Ecclesiae,"* all according to the Mind of the Church. We went to Rolly's room, and I read the questions out in a kind of disembodied, authoritative voice, as I thought they demanded, and it was uncomfortable, all about whether or not Rolly believed he had ever truly had a genuine Vocation to the religious life, whether or not he had acted sincerely and in good faith, whether or not he had concealed anything. Rolly in turn answered in the loud, clear voice of good conscience. As the Dispensation proceeded, I thought I could discern the personage of the one asking the questions; and even more, I felt that there were several, for I could tell when the Canon Lawyer of the Sacred Congregation for Religious handed the questioning over to the Dogmatic Theologian, and, finally, to the Moral Theologian. It was a kind of battle, a legal battle, or process. In order for the Dispensation to properly take place, the Petitioner had to make it clear that he was morally obliged to seek dispensation, and the "Lawgiver," he with the Mind of the Church, had to be satisfied that—as a "concession to human weakness," or because a well-intentioned error had been committed, or because of invincible human ignorance—the Church in its rectitude would be justified in loosening and untying the bonds that had been so firmly tied.

Question 116, I think it was, asked the Petitioner to circle the one word which best summed up any difficulties he might be having with sexual temptations against the Vow of Chastity. I read this question out straight-faced, in a kind of schoolmarm fashion, but when I saw that Rolly had circled the word "Unremitting" I thought I would begin to laugh and set Rolly off on one of his famous uncontrollable laughs. But the occasion was so serious we both held ourselves in.

Finished, Rolly took the Dispensation form from me and labored to write his name carefully in the little circle provided. Under the pressure of the moment, he made some kind of mistake, and rubbed it out and wrote it in a few times, in the process all but destroying the circle, so that some letters seemed to be pouring out of it.

Then Rolly wanted to be alone. There was five minutes before "Partic"—the Particular Examination of Conscience, which occurred each day at precisely 11:50 A.M., just before the noon meal. I went to the window in the main corridor and looked over the front lawns.

The bell for Partic rang, and my fellow seminarians

emerged from everywhere—library, Index room, Aula, rec room—to form two long lines in black, moving silently along, answering the Voice of God.

But there was a strange feeling in the air that morning, a nervousness belied by all that silence. I heard a rustle of paper behind me; it was Rolly, hurrying past. He bumped me, instead of air-brakes; he was on the way to the Superior's office to hand in his Dispensation; it was the last time I saw him.

Somehow, I swear, I felt I knew what was going to happen; somehow, I believe that everyone in the two long lines in black was instinctively ready for it, without ever being told. But Rolly, as he ran, deciding to chance it, to chance everything, threw his head back, and from his throat emerged a blood-curdling scream, which broke the sacred silence, shocked everyone, shocked A.J., who was already running next to him, but who threw his head back, too, and gave also the same wild, exciting, terrifying scream, which I recognized at once as their version of the Rebel Yell. I don't know who took it up next, but each one next in line joined in the foolish wildness, breaking silence irreparably, breaking the Rule, daring it almost certainly that they would be caught by superior authority moving toward Partic. I did it, too; not even knowing properly how to do it, I raised my head like Rolly and A.J. and let it out. Even Jim Blaes, who had been reciting his breviary, gave it a try. For an instant it echoed, a half-life of reverberation, Rolly running with his papers in his hand, A.J. running beside him. When they came to the old statue, the old Sphinx at the corner, Rolly twirled on its tail, as he often did, and headed toward the Superior's office. A.J. and the rest of us straightened up at the statue, turned right, and walked solemnly into the Chapel. No one was ever caught; for all I know, nobody but us ever heard our Rebel Yell. But that was the last we saw of Rolly.

II. Roma Locuta Est

Rev. Mr. Martin Gunther was distinguished; he wore a European greatcoat, and fondly told many times how the hostess at a function had remarked, "Why, you look like a Polish prince!" as she helped him on with it. Martin was convinced that a synthesis was possible between the modern thought of Sartre and Ortega y Gasset and the traditional thinking of the Church. I was annoyed at being pitted against him, for, though only in Third Theology, he was generally conceded to be the best theological mind we had. When he thought, he agonized, holding one hand out in front of his forehead as though he were clutching at the light of truth. He would go up *"Ad sinistram"* onto the podium that night, trying to find some exception to the stern thesis "Outside the Church there can be no salvation," carrying an armful of liberal publications and saying, "Ortega says . . ."

In the beginning we worked together as friends; but in the weeks before the *Disputatio* we stayed apart. For Martin it would be a formal exercise within his field of discipline. But in my case, after I had done the research that was necessary, each day brought me closer to the realization that for me it was no mere exercise. It was all coming down to one thing: whether I believed or did not believe all that the Church taught. Father Corkery had been right, he could see it in my face. And if he knew it, the House Council knew it. What was the use?—I knew it myself.

I began to spend time meditating—in the end, more time meditating than studying. The day of the *Disputatio*, late in the afternoon, I sat in the second pew on the Gospel side of the chapel, which was a splendid study in black-and-white marble rising to the solid black table on scrolled Bernini columns, nine steps in three sets which carried out the theme, even to the pewter candlesticks and the Tabernacle of silver upon the altar.

I decided to take the attitude recommended to me, that of the great Saint Anselm. There were certain difficult concepts which could not be comprehended except through religious faith: to understand their full force, you had to believe first. *"Credo ut intelligam,"* Anselm said; "I believe, in order that I *may* understand."

That afternoon, with all the sincerity that was in me, I said, *"Credo ut intelligam,"* by which I meant everything—my thesis, and the inflexible theology of the Church on Error, and whatever else was necessary to the making of a good priest.

"Credo ut intelligam," I repeated; then I rose, got down on my knees in a double genuflection, bowed to the Tabernacle, and went off to the *Disputatio*.

I had made one other decision very early. In my arguments I would restrict myself not to what certain Theologians said, or even what tradition said, or what had been uttered in minor Episcopal chapters; no, I would simply, at the peril of sounding machine-like, restrict myself solely to the utterance of those theses which had been infallibly defined in the Councils of the Church. I would, as far as it was humanly possible, simply let Holy Mother Church speak for herself.

The *Disputatio* followed a strict form. A kind of Master of Ceremonies—we irreverently used to call him the Interlocutor—stated the thesis once, clearly, in Latin. You rose, repeated it, and then listed, also in Latin, *"Ad primum," "Ad secundum," "Ad tertium"*—usually three main objections which historically had been made to it. Then, *"Sed contra"*—on the contrary—saying, *"Respondeo dicendum,"* you read a brief Defense of Thesis, in Latin which had been carefully edited with the help of the Classics professor. You replied to each objection, and concluded with your ringing *"Ergo"*:

"Ergo: *Extra Ecclesiam Christi, nulla salus!"* Outside the Church, there is no salvation.

The other side presented its case in similar format. After a pause for a sip of water, the two disputants pulled out everything they had in an impromptu discussion, a heated discussion mostly in Latin but often in English, full of *"a fortiori"* and *"Secundum quid"* and "I beg to differ" and *"Nihilominus."* The floor was then thrown open to everyone in the amphitheater—from the rest of the faculty to visitors from the university campus. There was a final summation, then everyone retired to the soiree.

Martin and I waited in the darkness, in a side room, like actors waiting for the play to start. Schunermann, my friend with me to the last, kept peeking out between the curtains to see "what kind of a house" I had. Suddenly he said, "Holy shit! There's Cicognani! The *Apostolic Delegate* is here! Amleto Giovanni Cicognani! You poor bastard—'*Amleto*'—you've got *Hamlet* sitting in the front row!" And he went out into the corridor so that he could laugh out loud. Martin and I were called to the center of the Aula stage, bowed to the Delegate, and mounted the platform, one to each side.

It was, in the end, easy; I needn't have worried so. The Divine Armory of the Church, twenty centuries of Universal Councils, from Nicea in 325 A.D., to Ephesus and Jerusalem, on to Florence and Lyon and Trent and, finally, in our own time, to the Vatican, their canons set indefectibly, forever, against Error and its victims— "Those misguided by Erroneous opinions, whom Discord keeps aloof"—stated irreversibly and beyond all doubt what everyone present had already known: that no one ever had been saved, and that no one ever could be saved, outside of the One True Church.

Poor Martin. Hamlet clutching a light bulb, he kept up the fight. He conceded the Major—he had to, for it was a Dogma of the Church—"*Concedo Majorem*," he would say, but "*Sed distinguo—distinguo. . . .*" And then, wildly searching through Sartre, and thumbing over copies of *Commonweal* magazine, he kept making distinctions: that the Church existed for Man, not Man for the Church, that it was the Divine Will that all men should be saved, and so on and on. "*Concedo . . . Concedo . . . ,*" he kept saying, "*sed distinguo.*" And when he tried to push all troublesome doctrines into the dim and distant past, asserting that the Church had in modern times surely moved on "beyond medieval practices," I quoted the Vatican Council from the very period in which we lived:

Vatican Council 7:196.

It is a Dogma of Faith that no one can be saved outside the Church. If anyone is not in this Ark when the flood rages, *he will perish*. The Council rejects that irreverent doctrine of religious indifferentism by which the Children of this World, failing to distinguish between Truth and Error, say the gate of eternal life is open to anyone, no matter what his opinion. *On the contrary, they are consigned to Darkness and to Belial*. Anathema Sit!

None of these things finished him off, however; it was something else. There was a point, after an extended amount of such citations, at the very heart of the *Disputatio*, where I saw him give up. It had little to do with the logic of the argument itself; I saw it happen, it was at the words *"Mit brennender Sorge"* that I kept repeating, the "With burning care" and "Fiery concern" of Pius XI to the German Church, along with the four hammer blows of Boniface VIII declaring that all human creatures must be subject to the Roman Pontiff for Salvation:

> *declaramus,*
> *dicimus,*
> *definimus*
> > *et* pronunctiamus!

Merely the very sound of the words seemed to call forth for Martin what we both knew: that no matter how brilliantly he sought to find expression for his side of the argument, the preponderant mass of Church statement was on my side, and it in the end would be overwhelming.

We both quit at that moment. He restated his position and sat down. With a flair for the dramatic, I simply strode forward out to the front of the platform, out into the light of the footlights, and pronounced with great clarity the words

> *Roma locuta est—*
> *Causa finita est!*

There was applause; and all retired to the soiree.

After it was over, old Father "Pops" Condon, who could be relied on to shout something at every meeting, shouted out, "Good work, Father! You gave us what Saint Paul call 'the rational milk, without guile'! Solid stuff!" Ray Cour asked if he could have my sources, he was so impressed. But as I moved away I heard Father Chet Soleta say to someone, "That was nothing new. All he did was repeat the *Unam Sanctam* decree!" No fool, I moved off.

"Ice cream!" said Mister Knous to me. "Have some dessert! My God, you demolished him!"

"*Ad multos annos!*" a voice said at my elbow, and instead of the ice cream I was handed a large, delicate glass of red wine: it was Mister Markos—we were having wine that night. I tasted it—it was delicious, the first alcoholic beverage of my adult life except for drinks we had snitched in the cellar. Mister Markos said, "Father Corkery sent it. He said for me to say, '*Ad multos annos*,' and that you would know what that meant."

I didn't get back to Martin that night; he was sur-

rounded by his friends. Father Corkery I saw across the
room; he was eating jujubes; he looked pleased.

After my victory, the last month of the seminary was
essentially waiting for ordination and, of course, waiting
for my chalice. I lolled nervously, listening to music,
popular songs, mostly, and, with new privilege, the radio.
"He's going back to the Bull Pen!" shouted the voice of
Mel Allen, "He's gonna go to his Bull Pen!" announcing
some meaningless Yankee baseball game, reminding me
of when I was a child on Dunlap Street. "Yes, Ladies and
Gentlemen, believe it or not, he's going to the bull pen!
How about that? How 'bout dat?" And Gillette Blue
Blades for a super shave, look sharp, feel sharp, along
with the Tennessee Waltz, Blue Tango, and "Vaya con
Dios, My Darling." And in the very last weeks, "Little
Things Mean a Lot," with Eddie Fisher singing "I'm
Walking Behind You."

We played word games, Ghost and Super-Ghost, where
you had to add a letter in the proper spelling of something, or lose. Our games mined the vastness of Dogma
and Moral, with words like "Antinomian" and "Patripas-
sian" and "Bogomil" and "Consolamentum" and "Mol-
linist." Schunermann won one game with "Amplexus-
reservatus," a hyphenated word which I disputed but
which McInerny allowed, and I had to get back at them.

One afternoon in the recreation room, listening to
Eddie Fisher singing "O My Papa," playing the game
with Schunermann and McInerny again, it was my turn
to add a letter to "ph." Almost any letter would give the
game away. Sitting there watching Schunermann sucking
on his enormous cigar, enjoying life too much, I calmly
said, "Y before P."

Schunermann sat up, took his cigar out of his mouth, and said, "Y before P? Y before P? Yph? You gotta be a reetard! There's no Y before P!"

"Challenge him," said McInerny. "There is no such word."

"I challenge you! What's your word?"

"Ithyphallic."

Schunermann took out a piece of paper and asked me to spell it for him. Then he went upstairs to look it up in the library. He was gone a long time.

"Pull the chain," he was saying as he returned. He handed the scrap of paper to McInerny, on which was written:

"Ithyphallic: having an enormous penis, shaped like a fish." I won the game, but there was a tremendous commotion in the stairway: Scoop Laurick had arrived breathlessly. "Package from Germany!" he was shouting. "Domgoldschmiedehaus! Domgoldschmiedehaus Schwartzmann!" And he came to me and said, "Your chalice has arrived."

All four of us rushed up to the parlor. Laurick helped open it, first pink-and-blue cotton with the scent of sandalwood rising and the shine of metal: perfect. Breathtaking. Just as I had asked for, the very thing I had drawn in blueprints over and over, to the last gauge of micrometer. The ineffable Trier artisans of the Rhineland had done it again, just as they had for Rheims centuries before. The gold cup, the black onyx, the chased silver, and—I looked—the chrysoprase from my father, and there my mother's wedding ring. A crowd gathered, and someone said, "It's the best yet. It's the best of all of them."

Schunermann never forgave me. He let a respectable amount of time lapse after the arrival of my chalice, but at supper, after the Reading of the Rule, he shouted, "Ithy-*what?*" The whole refectory heard him, and for the next few weeks, until ordination, I heard people all over the House saying, "Ithy-what? Ithy-*what?*"

In the end he was very proud of me.

"DIENBIENPHU HAS FALLEN!" the headlines said one May morning. "THE FALL OF DIENBIENPHU," "DIENBIENPHU FALLS" on all the tables of the priests' recreation room. I couldn't wait to get to them later, so I made an excuse— to re-supply the cigarettes—getting into the room during midmorning break, and I read all of them. The names Christian de Castries, General Navarre, General de Lattre were mentioned. It talked about the Plain of Jars, being caught in a noose, how the French artillery had been out-dueled by the guerrilla artillery of the Communists, how the flower of French chivalry had fallen and been taken captive. The Last Outpost of the West, the paper said.

Dienbienphu. The very word was like a bell. Perhaps that was what it meant; it was translated as the Place of the Last Boundaries. An American general was quoted, saying that it was "the key to Hanoi and the Mekong Delta," and that it should not have fallen. He mentioned the need for "superior fire-power" and "improved air-drop capability." I remembered the eighteen Grumman Bearcats trundling backward through the jungle, and the picture I had seen in in our foreign Mission magazine of a French cathedral with the Red Flag down its façade, and I wondered what would come next. Senator McCarthy was right, no question now about the size of the tragedy. Dienbienphu. That week I went off to the last of my classes with the name of the place ringing in my head; to this day I cannot hear it without thinking of funeral bells, and of death itself.

But there was still one piece of unfinished business. On Tuesday of the last week I went to the tailor to pick up my new clerical black suit. Wednesday I got dressed up in it with a neat, military-type Roman collar, and I went with the young men in the cab for the last time to Saint Elizabeth's. I visited for a while with Ruth Wolfewitz at the Registrar's office, and then headed over to Howard Hall to say goodbye to what was left of my choir.

My last day at Howard Hall was not much different from any others: I was locked in and could not get out. I had the keys, but they would not work. Male keys for a female lock, then female keys for a lock turned male. And all keys too old for too-old locks, no teeth, no anything, turning round like wood in steel. A hand came down on my shoulder from behind and fear went through my body. But it was only "Walt Whitman" in his steel jockstrap: Brother, don't you have the keys? Isn't that a key chain around your waist? Do not be afraid. You could escape! You could escape us both!

I thanked him, but moved him back, majestically: I had already said my goodbyes and wanted to slip away. But Antonelli's wild green eyes saw my predicament. "Brother! They lock you in?" He came over and hurled his weight against the door, shouting, "Jackson! Open up the fuckin' door! You locked the Brother in! Open up this fuckin' thing or I'll bust it out!" and he started kicking it on the bottom while I kept trying keys. Stacey came up at once, he knew how the keys worked, and almost had them out of my hands; I pulled them back and he said, "Well, then gimme a rosary, then!" And as I reached with my free hand into my pocket and felt for one last string of beads I saw someone I had not seen in a long time: Stickles, poor old Stickles, poor old Clyde, back from surgery, huge hands out in front like a jagged lobster now, feeling his way along too-difficult hallways to say goodbye; I had forgotten him.

"I will touch the door," said General Custer in his frontier outfit. "I will touch the door should you but ask!" and with my free hand I reached over and held Stickles' hand in mine. "Father Wheeler will be here," I promised him, "You'll have someone—he's permanent." *"Open the door, open up the fuckin' door!"* sounded in my eardrum, and I found one last string of beads in my suit pocket, with a Miraculous Medal attached to it. "No," shrieked Stacey, "It's *my* rosary, you promised!" And I told him to take the medal off and give it to Stickles, but to keep the string of beads for himself. There was a scuffle, Antonelli holding Stickles away while Stacey worked on the little links and a foot kept booming against the door. "Do not be afraid," I heard Whitman say, then General Custer in an elaborate gesture reached over my head, touched the door, and it clicked open: Jackson had arrived. I was let out; the last I saw was Stacey running back into the ward with the string of beads over his head; I hoped Stickles had got the Miraculous Medal.

"Take keer a these guys," said Jackson, slamming the door; he had been drinking.

Then I went to see Ezra Pound.

"What are you *doin'* in that crazy black suit?" he demanded as I came up the steps. "You're crazier than *I* am!" he shouted. "I'm crazy, I *have* to be in this shithouse! You don't! Git out of the shithouse!"

I tried to change the subject, to talk of other things. I

told him my chalice had come, about the black ivory node. *"Ebur,"* he said, *"eburneus."*

I said something which I hoped would please him; I said I thought my chalice was something better than "a Roman copy of a Greek original." He smiled, but shook his head. "You have some distance ahead of you," he said, "a long way and that's the truth, like the man said. You better look to your ships! *Subito!* SUBITO *subito!"* And with that he turned to someone who had been waiting for him, a distinguished person, undoubtedly, from the world of literature. That was the last I saw of Ezra Pound.

I walked to the Chaplain's office for the last time, past P Building, deliberately. "Cock-roach! Cock-roach!" came down. She had spotted it, too, my new black suit. "Buggeratzi!" she shouted. "Buggeratzi!"

"Last time!" I shouted up. "Last time! I'm going!"

"Good-bye" came down from between the bars.

On the last Thursday of May the last class was held— for some of us, the last class of eleven years of sitting on benches, taking notes, preparing for exams. Nothing could stop us now, we could no longer fail a course. As the House was cleaned that Saturday, the priests in their recreation room kept hearing noises coming from the trash chute, which had an opening there. Every few minutes a great weight would come hurtling down from the upper floors of the building.

It was Schunermann's turn to be houseboy that week, and so he was in the rec room. He told me what happened. After three particularly weighty and tumultuous thumps, Father Joe Rehage said, "I am going to see what that is!" He went over to the trash door, opened it, and peered in. "Why, it's my Canon Law notes!" he shouted.

"They're throwing out Sabbetti-Barrett! They're throwing out Prummer! They're throwing out *Woywood!*"

Schunermann laughed and laughed as he imitated Rehage whining the name: "*Woy*wood! They're throwing out *Woy*wood!" But he would not let me interrupt. "Then Father Paul Schrantz went over to the bin. He looked in, and *picked out a certain person's Dogma notes.*" Schunermann's eyes twinkled delightedly. "All four years of them, bound together with bindery twine. This person's name was clearly written for all to see." I agonized as he talked. "And most *profusely* illustrated, it was. Down every margin of every page was this endless *chain,* this endless *embroidery* of—let's face it, *doodles*— the intertwined boredom of four years." Schunermann was rollicking, almost unable to finish, paying me back for "ithyphallic" and everything else. "—And you know what he said? He followed the design up one page and down another, up the next and down that, noticing how it continued through all four years of every course. Then, with two fingers, like this, he held it up out of the garbage for all the other priests to see, and then he said, 'And what is this supposed to be? The Golden Thread of Catholic Thought?' Then, BONK, it went back into the trash bin with the rest!"

I grimaced painfully; and Schunermann added, "You should have heard some of the things the other priests said!"

"*Ecce Sacerdos Magnus!*" the choir shouted through the vast nave. I stood at the door of the East Transept; the moment of my life had arrived. Our college was first, out of custom, and behind me stood the rest of the *ordinandi,* from all the other colleges; 368 young men from all over the country. Each of us held a Dalmatic folded in front of him, made by his mother or some devout woman, and had looped over his cincture two strips of linen string, the *panniculi*. At the word *"Jurejurando,"* Father Schutz, Master of Ceremonies for the National Shrine, nodded to me and hissed, *"Ad sinistram!"* To the left. And we processed to the altar, prostrating ourselves before the Bishop's throne.

I had been so afraid that the moment would not come, or that when it did I might actually miss it by oversleeping, that I had set two alarm clocks the previous night, and asked Bill Swiercz and Jerry Jones to double-check me to see if I was awake. Both laughed at my concern, but both did as I had asked.

Everyone was there. Father, Mother, all my relatives, friends, some not of the Faith. The Sisters who had fed us all those years were there in their white and blue, and our Superior, and all our professors.

Ordination is dramatic. The ordaining Bishop asks a series of questions in Latin: Do you know what it is that you are doing? It is very difficult; can you do it? Are you doing this of your own free will? Will you honor your vows before the Lord, *in perpetuity?*

Finally, the Bishop states clearly that if there is any one among the *ordinandi* who knows that he ought not to be ordained, he should, in the name of God, depart. There is a long pause. Then the names are called, in alphabetical order. Each of those to be ordained, when his name is called, answers *"Adsum,"* present. I stood rockfast, I was certain.

That moment, along with the anointing and laying on of hands, constitutes ordination, after which there is no turning back: it is done.

"Richardus Atwater?" Father Schutz called out. "*Adsum!*" came the clear response.

"Fredericus Barr?"

"*Adsum.*"

"Guglielmus Brown"

"*Adsum.*"

"Hieronymus Jones"

"*Adsum.*"

They say I crouched like a runner waiting for the starter's pistol, and I know I silently recited each name to myself as they came in alphabetical order. I had some wild fear that my throat would not work, that I would forget the sound of my own name, that there had been a typographical error. When my name came down from the altar, I shouted back, "*Adsum,*" so loud there was a stir out in the congregation. I didn't care; getting it out was the one thing that mattered. It must have been as they said, for afterward Bishop Sheehan shook my hand and said, "You really wanted to make sure, didn't you, Father!"

What I remember. At my first Mass, walking up the altar steps with my biretta on, and Hurley hissing to me, "Take off your hat!" but after that blunder, feeling relieved, I began saying the Mass. Until, at Consecration, I leaned over the Host like all priests do, but even more over the Chalice: knowing above all that, it was not me, really, that it was Christ who was the real minister of the Sacrament. "*Hoc est enim, Hic est enim calix sanguinis mei.*" I had succeeded. I had not drowned at Black Water. God *had* called me after all, unbelievably, redeeming the time, redeeming all those in the church, those born and dead before me, those unborn and yet to come, those out in the nave, my relatives, my own mother and father, a priest taken from among men. I being validly ordained, the words, the form, the matter had their strength, no matter what else happened now; everything was saved. And Schunermann an altar boy, not laughing now. No, not at this. No jokes here, no jokes about his own desire to be where I was.

To be where I was. And most of all I remember Billy. And most of all, Lord, we remember Thy servant Billy, all covered with clay, who is not present this morning, under the appearance of bread and wine. Swear. Of course. The wedding ring flashes, and the chrysoprase, as it passes my eyes as I raise the chalice of all my work, all my years of beating—beating exams, beating Corkery, enemies, my own self to become this, to elevate it so, up high enough that people can see it, not wobbly. And down, and genuflect before it. Domgoldschmiedehaus.

And back in Pittsburgh, waiting in the Sacristy for my first Solemn Mass, the same Sacristry where I had lit the incense so many times, and had fought with Ray Bergman over who would take the book or the bell. Father Pat, my uncle, sent over to represent the relatives in Ireland, stood beside me. We made small talk: what did they thing of Senator McCarthy in Ireland? "We thought he was doing a good job until he let that Boston lawyer, that Welch fellow, pull his crying act!" I looked out through the curtain; Jean Marie Mangan would not be there; she had gone to the convent before I had gone away to be a priest.

And in the Confessional, too, later that week. Sure, I would help out, glad to, with my new faculties. And back in the box, the same Confessional box I had clung to that day I had lied to God, to Father O'Connor (May he rest in peace). Sweet young girls' voices, old grumbles, bad breath, with Joné in my pocket for consultation in the dark: turn to page 253 for Internal Forum before you lose the sinner. And one young boy, his mind excited by what he had seen that week, came not to confess, but to confide: he, too, wanted; he, too, like me, just like me, same problems, same deliriums, same girlfriend. Of course, Son; go thou and do likewise; but it is difficult. Study hard.

After that, my first airplane flight (as seminarians we had not been allowed to fly): a rickety old Lockheed Constellation, reeking of gasoline, shaking surprisingly and vibrating on the runway, but climbing up over the coal tipples of Pittsburgh, and banking toward Washington again for my first assignment. So this was flying?

My first duty was conducting a funeral at Arlington National Cemetery for a Navy pilot killed in an accident. I was inexperienced: the young, handsome body, shipped back from the Pacific, was sealed and bolted under glass. The young widow, wild with a desperate last effort to help him, said, "But he doesn't have his rosary! Father, he always had his rosary! Father, get them to put his rosary beads in his hands!" I looked at the young body secured by rivets under glass, and wondered wildly with the young woman: perhaps they could, maybe we could get them to open his prison just a crack, so that she could slip in to him her string of *Ave*'s and promise of eternity? Over her shoulder the undertaker was gesticulating wildly, his face distorting into a rage at the utter impossibility. He gestured to someone, and the black lid came down on the coffin, devouring him forever. And we were off to Arlington, the Honor Guard in silver helmets, and the procession. I was last, the Chaplain, just in front of the gun carriage bearing the downed pilot. The big horses pulling the gun carriage were immediately behind me. I kept looking around, because going uphill they labored slowly, but coming down I heard their furious hooves moving faster and faster at my back as they labored against the weight of the gun carriage, and I could not help looking behind me. And in the end, of course, the commanding officer gave the young widow her flag.

That's all. I was a dedicated priest, full-time and no nonsense. I left the priesthood twenty-one years after ordination, thirty-two years after first ringing the doorbell at the Little Seminary, but while I remained I did a good job. Sometimes in the Confessional, but more often in the classroom, for I taught literature. Always, though, I was available for priestly duty, sliding back and forth the little wooden panel doors on countless Confessionals, from G Street in Washington to Battleground in Oregon, to New Buffalo, Michigan, Flatbush, Brooklyn, Saint Patrick's on Fifth Avenue, and of course, Sacred Heart, Notre Dame.

In the fifth year of my priesthood, on the weekend of the Fourth of July, I was called back with my entire class for something called a "Renewal Program"—back to the old camp in the mountains.

We had never expected to see it again, never thought to be together as a group again. There were whoops of laughter, and nicknames shouted and stories being told.

I had hardly said hello to anyone, hardly sat down at table for the first camp lunch, when Father Laurick came up to me with the urgent message, "Father, your mother is dying."

We were closer to Pittsburgh, everyone said, but the roads to Washington were faster. The only way out, though, was the old truck, brought down from the farm in Indiana; if I could drive that, if I could handle it, I could drop it off at Washington Airport and be home by the end of the day. Moose Mulcahy stopped me; he was carrying a load of tentpoles and pegs. "You leavin' us?" he asked. I tossed my bags on, Charlie Wallen helped adjust the rear-view mirrors, and I lurched off, in first gear; I found out later that you start an empty truck in second. It was all clutching and shifting for the first half-hour; the noise of the engine astonished me, and when I got it up to speed and really made time, the fencing on the back clattered and clattered.

III. Son of Man: Prophesy

"JORDAN RUN," "DORCAS," "LOST CITY," "LOST RIVER." Town names rushed by, but no towns to go with them.

Dying? From what? Maybe only seriously ill. We could pray. "The secondary effect of the Sacrament of Extreme Unction is cure of the body." (Dorenzo, the *Res et Sacramentum.*) Headwaters of the Youghiogheny, headwaters of the Potomac—we rushed down to their little iron bridges, then climbed up the other side. "MOUNT NEBO CHURCH ROAD," said one of them, and the truck went slowly. Dorcas, back there, I thought—Dorcas? I remem-

bered. In Greek it means gazelle, from Scripture. Everything in the country was named for the Bible. Suddenly
in the slow roar it came to me: Tabitha and Dorcas were
the same name, for a girl: "Tabitha, come forth! Tabitha,
arise!" Jesus working a miracle? No, not Jesus . . . someone later. *Peter*—Peter trying out his new powers. "And
the woman came forth." The settlers had known it, had
seen a deer or something come down from the Alleghen-
ies, and said, We will call the place Dorcas, Gazelle. Or
worse: someone had died, a settler's wife, and they
prayed: Tabitha, arise. And they prayed—if she would
not arise in this world, then another. They knew the
whole Bible, better even than Jo Mac's Scripture course.

Would she be there? Up Mount Nebo the engine
repeated my word: there? there? there? Anything I said
or thought, any name, if I let it, the great rackety hurtling
truckbed threw back at me, had a sound for, as though it
were a breathing monster.

At the top the engine stopped laboring, we coasted
out into a large, gentle curve, and there it was, the Valley
of the Shenandoah. The beautiful, the beautiful river.
At Moab there was a turnout for viewing, and it looked
as though you could see to Lynchburg in its plain, beyond
Harper's Ferry, to the Atlantic Ocean itself, but I could
not stop.

Down through the Shenandoah Valley, through the
Civil War towns the fencing on the back sang as I hurried.
Her songs came back to me: "Charming Billy," "Birming-
ham Jail," "Molly on the Shore," "The Red River Valley," and they became mixed with those Dick Gorman
had led us in, on the back of the truck—"Swing Low,
Sweet Chariot," "The Walls Come Tumbling Down,"

184

and "Someone's in the Kitchen with Dinah." Gorman
had already managed to leave the priesthood, the first of
all those of us who were to go, and his figure rose up
pomading his hands as he led us on the back of the truck
in Wisconsin, on the back of the truck in Michigan, and
in Maryland, singing "Oklahoma!" and "Old Butter-
milk Sky," and "On Top of Old Smoky," and of course
his song, "This Was a Real Nice Clambake."

"CULPEPPER 24," said a sign, and another pointed
toward Stonewall Jackson's Headquarters; there were
other signs for Frederick and of course the Shenandoah
River itself. I stopped at a place called Salem Church,
and a slow black hotel barman came out to me; he was
kind as he said he would mix me something I would like,
a Horse's Neck, a mixed drink with a lemon peel looking over the rim like a foal looking over the fence at you,
and a sandwich on whole wheat. He brought it out to me
between huge ante-bellum columns, on a silver service,
with slow black hands. I told him the reason for my
hurry, and as I gulped, he spoke of peace, and of eternity.
He promised me she would be there. The last word he
shouted after me as I rushed on was "Forever": I was one
more Yankee who understood neither time nor life, and
he was gone, with Salem Church.

The early-afternoon heat of the valley, together with
the one hurried drink, and the fumes from the engine,
and the endless repetition of sounds from the back of the
truck, each of which became a word, had a hypnotic
effect which I did not like. I wanted only to think of her.
I tried to stave it off, but it would not work. I had no
sooner seen the word "ANTIETAM" on a sign than it all
began: the truck picked it up and for miles all we heard

was "Antietam" over and over, until its place was taken by "Shiloh-Shiloh-Shiloh" and I thought of the Wilderness. Possessed of these creatures, I might as well have been walking through the Bible itself: "And I came to a great valley full of dry bones and the Voice said to me, Son of Man, prophesy, can these bones rise again?" And the fencing said Again? Again? and there was no use putting it off, it would not be put off a hundred times, until (Cowpens, it said) I conceded and gave in and knew I would be accompanied as I always was for hours by whoever it was going to be. Who was it? Who was it, who was it, who was it? (Will she still be there?)

I looked through the rear-view mirror to see if there was a trooper behind me, at seventy-two mph. There was not. There is, however, an officer of another stripe, and suddenly I know who he is, I know who is saying these things. He is a Confederate, that old Tennessee veteran, old Eli Browning's Confederate, the one that spoke once, that old officer; the one they asked to speak at a banquet years later, after the War. They got him up after the meal and someone said, Do it please for us, can you do it once, just give it, we have heard so much about it but have not heard it itself, can you give us the old Rebel Yell?

And the old Confederate, steadying himself, standing at attention, standing at the banquet table. *Why do you disturb my rest?* he asks.

The Rebel Yell! we answer; we want to hear the Rebel Yell! Come on, we fed you, give us a shout, they say you can do it. We ask it fervently, and with respect; we lived afterward; we never heard it. The yell, please; that is an order, Sir.

And he rose before them and he says, what does he say?

* * *

IT IS IMPOSSIBLE, he says.
 We do not know what it is we ask.
IT WOULD BE IMPOSSIBLE TO GIVE THE REBEL
 YELL
—IT IS IMPOSSIBLE UNLESS MADE AT A DEAD
 RUN
—IN FULL CHARGE
                —AGAINST THE ENEMY.

IT WOULD BE AN ERROR;
NOT ONLY CAN IT NOT BE GIVEN
               IN COLD BLOOD
STANDING STILL,
BUT IT WOULD BE WORSE THAN FOLLY TO
 TRY TO IMITATE IT
WITH A STOMACH FULL OF FOOD
AND A MOUTH FULL OF FALSE TEETH.

No one clapped. The truck fencing picked it up and
hurled phrases back: It is impossible, it shouted—impossible! And An Error, and folly, folly, folly.

She was old; her own false teeth would be out in a
glass, the nurse having taken care of that, Father. I
stopped for gas.

Continue. You were saying. You will say anyway, will
say on until I dump this thing and get into the air and
fly.

*The Wilderness. I was in the Wilderness and saw them
die.*

*When we broke camp that morning everything was all
bright and blowy. We looked back to a softness of light
the world has never seen—all accounts square to that.
Many of us knew we would not return to it.*

Have you heard an army moving to battle? No; I had not. *It is a sound unlike any other; once you have heard it, you can tell it miles away. Of all the battles, Shiloh was the worst, Sherman says, and he should know, it was the first big one, that said they had a war.*

But it was not like the Wilderness! The dogwoods were in blossom. Have you seen the dogwood in flower?

I have, in Virginia, easing the spring, more beautiful than the Tidal Basin cherries, than the black Flowering Judas of the Midwest, even. In the dark forest when nothing else seems alive, they appear from nowhere, you cannot tell you have one until it bursts, then you have everything on your hands, like springtime, the smell of existence. She is still alive; she will be there.

I looked back to reassure myself; speeding, there was no officer behind me. *But it was not like the Wilderness! In the deep forest no one knew who they fought. You fired where the most noise came from. The wounded lay on the forest floor, which caught fire, exploding the cartridge belts around their ribs and around their waists, causing terrible wounds. A surgeon cut off arms and legs at Spotsylvania Courthouse for two whole days, and then for four days more, and he had no time for chest wounds. Bullets clipped branches, which came down steadily, like rain; there was smoke from guns and smoke from the fire of the burning forest, and when the light of heaven would break through, it would find the dogwood trees, lighting them up like creatures from heaven. They floated upon the air like the Angel of Resurrection, like angels with wings extended before the throne of God, and sometimes in the darkest pit of battle they looked like horrors; I fired at one. The Wilderness was forty days altogether;*

the dogwood came out in the pitch of battle and lasted most of it, until the trees, too, were cut down, and consumed, like everything else.

We're getting there: Lynchburg; begins to sound like Washington.

After the battle a reporter saw something: walking along the old plank road, he saw two bayonets sticking out across the road, pointing at one another, and in the ditch on either side, a Rebel boy and a Yankee boy, dead. They had both thrown themselves down, fired, and killed one another simultaneously.

Hell No. On the other hand, Shit Yeah. *Ho men—Ho day.* One side of the truck was saying to the other, arguing again; down through the Valley, down through the Valley of Bones: shall these bones rise again? Prophesy.

Hell No, one side would have the best of it for a while, Hell No, Hell No, Hell Noooooooooo until I got into a curve and I'd hear a long-drawn-out Sh——sh——shi ——yut Yeah! and another voice would shout, IT IS IMPOSSIBLE, IT WOULD BE IMPOSSIBLE, AND WORSE THAN THAT, FOLLY, mouth full of false teeth, Shit Yeah, out of some West Virginia hollow, up a hill, laboring Shit Yeah, Shit Yeah, like a mule train of Twenty Mule Team borax out in the desert, *Death Valley Days.* And at the top, Hell No. And all through it Dick Gorman on the back singing endlessly "This was a real nice clambake, We're mighty glad we came."

"MANASSAS JUNCTION 5." Bull Run all over again, where the Rebel Yell was first heard. My Confederate lay back, closed his own eyes, the way they do. Many are the hearts that are weary tonight. He didn't even ask me to fix him. "CAPITAL AIRLINES," "FLY EASTERN," the signs said. I dumped the truck, the last I ever saw of it, and was in Pittsburgh by seven.

I paid the cab fare outside her hospital in the intense Pittsburgh heat. And the extra bed the Sisters allowed me in the Maternity Emergency Ward: "But you better be ready, Father, you may be wakened in the night!"

I rushed in, and was shown down the corridor to her by the family. I put my head next to hers and kissed her. She saw me and said, "Are there clean sheets on your bed?" I thought, She thinks we are home, she does not understand anything, and I told the family, She thinks I am back home on a visit. But now I understand; forced to think of this again, I finally grasp it: she was telling me, "I looked after your bed always, now this bed is mine. Do it right."

I did. Thank God, I did. For three days I said over her first the prayers for the sick, the family spread out, starting with me, her priest, at the bedside, stretching past my sisters out to my brother in the hall outside her room, with his wife. My father sat up in a hospital chair in the corner the entire time. Then there was the operation, and the recovery room, cold and white with the hum of many motors.

She came back to us much diminished, and we increased our prayers. We were a nuisance to the hospital that long Fourth of July weekend: the young priest and his family refusing to let their mother die. I was the worst, shouting into her ear, for I wanted her to hear! At first I shouted beautiful things at her from the Psalms, and the *Collectio Rituum*: "My soul longs for the courts of the Lord, *Sicut Cervus*. As the Heart seeks after the water-brooks, so does my Soul long for Thee, O my God!" How beautiful, and as I prayed I knew it was all true. If I got the intention right, and got the words right (the form), since I was (and I was certain of this) a validly ordained priest of Christ, the anointing of Bishop's power going back in unbroken like to the Apostles, then the words of the Absolution would be successful, and the work of the anointing. But as we kept shouting, Doctor Fischelson, her doctor, had to tell me. "Father," he said and in his embarrassment dropped his pen in the corridor. "Father," he said again, coming up, "I do not have to tell you—we are both experienced in matters such as this—but she is *old*, Father—your mother is *dying*." But I would not hear, and rushed back in to absolve her once again.

At first I refused to anoint her; Extreme Unction was the Last Rites; she was not dying, not ready for that. Then I remembered: the secondary effect of the Anointing is Cure of the Body—Doronzo, Sacraments *in Genere*. And so I went to the hospital chapel and found them— the little vial with "O.I." on it, *Olea Infirmorum*, with little swabs packed in, well used in deaths, it was a hospital. And so I gave her the Divine Houseling of all her people from the beginning, the Holy Viaticum to accompany her on her way, and the Annaling, the Anointing.

First her tired pilgrim's feet. The feet may be omitted, the ritual said, for any rational cause and *"Si vivis,"* it said, "if you are living," before the formula. I decided to do it as it was in the book.

Si vivis, per istam sanctam Unctionem indulgeat tibi Dominus quidquid delequisti. Amen.

Someone helped me by picking up the sheet at the end of the bed, and I pressed my finger with the oil in a little cross on the sole of each foot. Cold, callused; all the way from Galway when she was a little girl on the beach; cold, bare feet of Irish kids. Pilgrim traveling light for eighty years; I anointed her for another journey.

She acknowledged nothing, and so for three days, from the First of July to the Fourth, I kept that whole wing of the hospital awake around the clock with my prayers for the dying, with endless, repeated absolutions. *"Ego te absolvo!"* I would shout again, until my old father from the back of the room finally complained out loud, "Why is he absolving her? She never did anything wrong." But I, you see, I wanted to make sure of one thing: that she died as she had lived, with her deep faith ever intact, so that Despair, black Despair would not creep in at the final moment between herself and that final brightness which she and all our people believed in from the beginning, and so I listened to no one, no, not to the nurse who braved the ire of the clergy to tell me to do it quieter, nor to Doctor Fischelson, who tried to tell me the truth, nor to my father, who said she didn't need it. I shouted and shouted so that, whichever moment it was, and whether I could tell it or not, she would hear in her dying ear at the moment of death what I knew she wanted to hear, my voice shouting after her, "Jesus! Jesus! My Jesus, mercy!" I did obey when the nurse said, "Take your head out of the tent, Father, you're using up her oxygen!" But I just shouted louder, outside the tent.

And so I did; I was there, her priest, shouting *"Ego te absolvo, in nomine Patris, et Filii, et Spiritus Sancti!"* and saying over and over, "Sacred Heart of Jesus, have mercy on me!"

For three days I shouted at her the Prayers for the Dying. As I looked at them, the words of the Church and

of Scripture were fearfully stark, and I had difficulty saying them: O Lord, hear my prayer, for all flesh comes
unto Thee. Why from the womb didst Thou draw me
out? From the womb to be transferred to the grave? I
should never have existed! I said in my excess, All men
are liars. How long, O Lord, wilt Thou suffer me to
swallow down my spittle? Dismiss me, O Lord, I will go
and not return, to a land *"tenebrosam,"* and covered with
the *"Mortis caliginem."* A land of misery and darkness
under the shadow of death where there is no peace, but
everlasting horror.

"A porta inferi": the Gates of Hell. The gates beneath,
I thought. What is beneath, what is above? True gates,
false ones. These bones shall exalt the Lord, the bones
that have been humiliated.

I wanted to shout out something else. I wanted to say,
"I will arise and come!" I wanted to sing *Sicut Cervus—*
My Soul longeth and fainteth for the Courts of the Lord!
But the terrible prayers went on and on, and I, Minister,
had to say them. Finally I came to the Song of Hezekiah,
from the Book of Isaiah:

> I said, I shall see the Lord no more in the land of
> the living.
> No more shall I behold my fellow men, those who
> dwell in the world.
> My dwelling, like a shepherd's tent, is struck down
> and borne away from me.
> Thou hast folded up my life, like a weaver who
> severs the last thread.

It got too much for me. I could not bring myself to
speak those words. My throat swelled up before I could

say, "No more shall I behold my fellow man" or "I am consigned to the gates of the nether world." And when I came to the words

> Thou hast folded up my life,
> Like a weaver who severs the last thread

I threw down the black old book, thrust my head into her oxygen tent, and shouted into each ear, "Jesus! Jesus! Merciful Jesus, have mercy on me!" And again I said the words of Absolution—*Ego te absolvo.*

I was delirious myself, trying to get the intention right, trying to keep the words right, carefully slipping a hand in, as the nurse had instructed, to form safely and correctly the cross within the confines of her tent.

I know it will sound untrue, as something that did not happen, but it is true: at last she opened her eyes, looked straight at me, and said, "I have heard every word you said!" Her face was contorted in a terrible spasm, and I knew at that moment she died. But as the books told me to, I kept shouting after her the words of her last anointing, her last houseling, for up to a half-hour.

As I came away, I felt a child again, abandoned on a shore; I thought of the thistle of childhood, blowing on the wind, rising, falling, then rising over the neighbors' house and gone.

On the way out I passed each member of the family; the last was my brother, out in the hall, my agnostic, unbelieving, critical brother, forever against my Vocation, my priesthood, and all else. He said, "I'm glad you did what you did. It is what she wanted, I am glad you did it." I nodded; it is one of the last things I remember talking to him about.

She had a worthy funeral. It simply is not done that way any more. The men came down from the summer camp with the last of it all: the Solemn High Mass of Requiem, sub-deacon, deacon, and priest moving in stately pomp to give this significant soul its departure. Crossing over, genuflecting, from Epistle to Gospel, with Lectors, Acolytes, Thurifers, and Exorcists, in ascending and descending orders, all the men from my class and those around it did the things they were ordained for, for the last time before it was changed: the old Latin, the old Greek, even the Hebrew at times, the Aramaic. And the choir, of course, it was still itself, for one last *"In Paradisum,"* one last *"Ego sum,"* one last *"Habeas Requiem."*

After it was over, Father Joe Stroot quietly said to me, "You know, Father, through it all I had the feeling we were burying more than your mother; I had the feeling we were burying Holy Mother Church Herself!"

She had died on the Fourth of July, and in the days after we buried her I heard the locusts telling that summer was over, that the summer's back was broken now, and that autumn was coming.

We brought my father home from the funeral and sat him down in the big old chair by the wall, and we went into the kitchen to prepare for the visitors who would be coming. But we were interrupted by a terrible groan from my father in the living room.

"Ohh," he groaned, " 'tis a lonely house now!"

There is not much more to say. I went home after that on vacations, for two summers, but it was not the same.

My father sat in his chair, saying his rosary, not talking much. I would paint, landscapes. He startled me one day with a request. Could I paint her? Couldn't I paint her, the way she was? She loved me. It would be the one thing that could please him. I said no. I could never do that. And he shook his head. He outlived her two summers.

I was a good priest, according to the rules of the priesthood itself. Twenty-five years of going into dark churches and even darker Confessionals. Sitting on the hard wooden bench, I managed never to send anyone away with their guilt upon them, always managed the Church's rules to say, "Your sins are forgiven. Go in peace."

Yet the strings of grass were flowing while I was not watching, streaming into little circles and whirlpools, breaking themselves up and forming new circles, played about by the wind on the surface of the deep, and finally I said No, I did not believe any more. But I was a good priest to the end, even to the questions of the Dispensation—which had now reached one hundred and seventy four. Answering them was the last thing I did *"ad mentem Ecclesiae."*

I still test the acoustics of strange places. When I am traveling, when I am in a motel shower, for instance, which reverberates, I hum the same four practice notes: "Hing—heng—hang—hunggg!" I take a deep breath—we are ready to begin. But nothing happens. There is no choir. *"Extra choram cantat,"* I hear a voice say, *"extra choram cantat."*

And I went back once, during a Christmas break, to the old House of Theology in Washington, to see if anything was left. There was nothing, it was gone, the Theologate had been pulled back to the Midwest in a retrenchment. The building was an Eye and Ear medical facility for the university.

It was so quiet when I got there that I thought it was closed for the holidays, but the marble main door, on its ancient system of rollers, opened silently as always. I looked for someone in the darkness, to ask if it was all right for me to be there. I could hear the sound of a typewriter, but could not find where it was coming from.

I did what anyone would do, I headed for the Chapel. It had been turned into offices, partitioned with plywood. I worked around the flimsy boards to get to where the sanctuary was, but the High Altar had been jack-hammered out, and the marble floor had been covered with green industrial carpeting. No six tall pewter candles, either. Perhaps they had been saved; perhaps they were in the Midwest, burning away.

I was pulled in every direction. The refectory was so black I could not see Bo Peep's window; the Aula Magna was locked, but I could see a stack of old newspapers, with a *Congressional Record* on top: "H.R. 1776," it said. My old room was gone, its walls knocked out to form a waiting lobby, though its window, with the same old fire escape, was still there. A sign said, "PARK A KID."

I could not help longing for something; I longed to resurrect them. In the main corridor I listened for the sound of air-brakes. "Chih-chih!" behind me, that would be Rolly Hunter, and then another "Chih!"—that would be A. J. Bates.

Resurrection. Yell them up, I said to myself, let it be as it was that morning on the way to Chapel, bright and blowy, when Rolly chanced it. I could see him throw his head back, I knew what was coming—infallible, certain:

he is a Confederate now, cassock a uniform of gray, we are already in long lines, anyway, to hurl ourselves. Rolly does it first, and from his throat emerges for the first time since Richmond, since Appomattox, that peculiar, terrifying cry so that I almost am scared, almost think it is real, and A.J., his next, takes it up at once; he knows what is going on, and then Buckley and Fahey and Shilts each to his next in line. I did it, too, knowing how to make it without ever having been told, how to place the tongue, how to hold the throat, for it comes to young men, certain young men, once every century or so, no one knows from where, and it echoes in the hallway, half-life of reverberation, an instant, opposite of Infinity, companions in blue, gray, shades of gray into blue/black, then finally turning beyond the statue of the Sphinx into the black darkness and silence at the Chapel door.

But they were gone. A.J. was a priest in Canada, but Rolly, they say, choked to death at table, laughing, laughing at everything, the way we were all afraid he might.

Nothing.

The Sphinx was still there, the only thing left; too heavy to move, apparently. Two tons, three? "On whomever it shall fall, it will grind him to powder."

I went around to the injury in its side, to the old lie, and put my hand into its side, to where the chisel marks were still new, the old cartouche broken, and the new one, ringing round the counterfeit, saying, "It is I; I will live forever."

I shook my head. I was annoyed; they were all gone, I alone was lingering there, spending my Christmas in a mausoleum. *"Fake,"* I said, and left.

I emerged into the warm Washington winter sun, and

felt I was coming out of a cave. I rolled the old block of
marble back over the entrance, and withdrew.

Responsibilities. Anne Francis. Life.

IV. All Gone into the World of Light

It is the Battle of the Wilderness surely, men themselves
exploding in the fire. Rain comes down, only it is not
water, of course, but clips of trees and branches descending. Those are General Buell's trenches behind us, are
they not, and that is holly shining as though out of season.
But who do we fight? Where is the enemy? Voices speak:
Odious things are to be restricted, *Res clamat ad Dominum,* Count no man happy. "Who owns our bodies?"
someone asks, and "What are people for?" Jo Mac appears
in a clearing: We have lost the Ark of the Covenant, he
announces, the Ark has been taken, is gone, and its
presence will not again be reported. Turn to your Ap-
pendix for the consequences. "It is impossible," I say,
"it is impossible." An enormous form rears up in front of
me, huge forearms raised to pounce, lit by unearthly
light. Fight back! I raise an unwieldy weapon I do not
understand, sluggish as in dreams as though bedclothes
or winding sheets hold back my arms, and I fire. It is a
dogwood tree in blossom, for it is spring, remember?

No, I am in error, for a choir sings. It is Echo Cove,
and voices waft like shades across the mists. The old *Ark*

drifts. The choir, dressed in war surplus, waits. It will be *Sicut Cervus*, one last time.

I hear the four notes, and wait for beauty to begin, but the words, cast up to the mountains, become chaos as though shouted by savages. *"Finita est"*—that's an old Indian phrase meaning nothing. All close their books quietly, the *Ark* glides off and is lost in the hollows of the opposite shore. It is the last I see, as though only a thin thread spun them to me.

My thread blows out across the waters; for a while it seems to shine in the sun, but the wind over the water thins it and thins it until I see that it is broken, and blowing free.

⏳ *EXODOS*

So, Semblable, so, Letter-Writer, all Nexts. My own nightmare. Paralysis of the moral act, cowardice, as I have been a coward once or twice, not this time. Caught doing what you know you should not do, or, rather, caught not doing what you should, not doing anything.

The long captivity, the growing old,
* banging our spoon against our bowl, screaming,*
*   That is not it!*
That is not what I meant at all!

Oh, it would have been easy. . . . Be quiet and do as you are told.

Cosseted, pampered; nurse, good nursing home; take your medicine, take it for us, will we take our bath, have we had our bath yet? Quiet wards, not madhouse, not insane asylum. Well cared for, even loved, but alcoholic perhaps. Looking at the Evening News. Alcoholic certainly.

I have read somewhere that sarcasm, irony, is the gift of those who feel themselves caught in a situation in which they are going to remain, from which they are not going to extricate themselves. I would have become gifted in irony; the bitter retort. And "sardonyx"—"the smile that tears the flesh," that distorts the face of the speaker.

Sphinxlike, our game discovered, found out, we turn upon ourselves, tear ourselves to pieces, destroy ourselves with long talons.

NO.

But you, Next. Dear Next! What is to become of you? Beware the long talons; I am sure you have long talons. Sarx, Sardonyx, smile tearing the face. And you smile; you will do nothing.

I think I know you. Someone I know but cannot place. . . . Someone very much like me . . . Someone long ago, dead now, who really no longer exists, the man with my face, my jokes, my number in its little circle. . . . Gone.

You plainly are going to do nothing. You will ask, and ask, and go on asking.

It makes me want to finish by my own Petition, an impossible prayer, to say what I cannot say, cannot ask.

Oh, Next, try
and free us from the nightmare
of the look back—the figure,
the all but empty clothes left purposely to scare us
waving
and hanging from the wire.

Soiree: Wild Mountain Thyme

"THIEF!" old Father John shouted at me. "You—are—a—
thief." He came over to the liquor closet, shouldered me
aside, and poured himself a large, very large, Wild Tur-
key, which was the only thing he ever drank. "All
thieves," he said, holding his drink up. "Thank God there
are a few of us left!" I got mine, and headed for the upstairs rec room, the place where we gathered for a late
last sup.

It always jolted me when he talked like that, and it took
me some time to figure it out. He meant that we were all
Unprofitable Servants, at best. "The only thing they let
you call your own are your sins!" he would say, taking
another swig. I think he got it from the Good Thief
hanging on the cross with Jesus, where he says to the
other thief: You and I are here for good reasons; but He,

what evil has He done? He turns to Christ and says, "Remember me, Lord, when Thou comest into Thy Kingdom." And Christ promises, "This day thou shalt be with Me in Paradise." It is in a beautiful Antiphon, *"Ait Latro ad Latronem,"* which we used to sing late at night on those few occasions when we all got drunk.

That night Father "Pete" Peterson was visiting us from the Midwestern Province; Father Pete was the one who, thirty-four years earlier, had answered my letter of inquiry at the Little Seminary, and he always regarded himself as my Sponsor; it was going to be quite a night.

You see, I had decided to leave. I had, quietly, stopped saying Mass, and steadfastly refused any priestly functions. I had leased an apartment, which I had not yet moved into, in the lovely Massachusetts town of Hingham, on the coast. There was no bed in it yet, only two pillows which I had taken from my cell upstairs, thinking that I was entitled to *some*thing after all those years. I had slept one night in it, reading the *New York Times* on my pillows under the lone hallway light, but, starting off with no money at the age of fifty, I was not anxious to be cut off from the House gasoline pump and, as I have indicated, the liquor cabinet. I was at the place where I was saying to myself, "Well, one more night can't make any difference."

We started early that night. Father John began saying "Pass the biscuits, Mirandy!" No one knew who Mirandy was, but when he said it he looked at me, and I knew he was going to get drunk. We started singing early that night, too, *"In Monte Oliveti,"* and *"Traditor Autem,"* and *"In Paropside"*—all songs of Holy Thursday, for some reason. Everyone came, and we talked about everything, about how the world and life and even the Church were changing, and how nothing was the same. Father John kept singing *"In Paropside"* off key, and getting louder and louder.

"These Young Turks!" Father John kept bawling out. "These Young Turks, they're living in *apartments* now! Living in *apartments*, mind you! I'd like to know what they *have* in those apartments! I'll bet they don't have the Blessed Sacrament in those apartments! They don't have the *Taber*nacle!"

There was laughter, because of the heavy stress he put on "Tabernacle," but it was easy to remember other nights he had gotten drunk and had shouted out things like "Hell, I'd like to get married, too! But look at me, *who'd have* me? *Who would have* me?"

"And the X's—" old Father MacSweeney from Ireland added, "—the X's is something else." He meant ex-priests. "They're stretching in a kind of arc," he said, his face contorted with a smile, "in a kind of arc, from Boston and Braintree all the way down to *Brock*ton! Brockton is a great place for them!" And he, too, lifted his drink to that.

The thought crossed my mind that maybe he knew something; I had set enough things in motion; soon people would know. . . .

Pete Peterson arrived with all the latest; in no time he was telling us what the Dutch theologians were saying about "Agape" and priesthood. It got pretty heated; Father John kept saying "The *priest's duty* is to con*fect* the Eucharist! The priest's duty is to *confect* the Euchar-ist!" and he would get another drink and come back and say it again. I remember at this point little Tommy Fiacre, a Reverend Mister on some form of assignment, sticking his head in the door, catching my attention, and saying, "Michigan! Michigan!" in warning that if we did not watch ourselves we were in danger of being sent back to the place in the Midwest where the order sent those who had trouble with alcohol.

I seized a quiet moment to ask my old sponsor, Father Pete, how his own priesthood was doing. "My priesthood? I have never been happier in it, never happier with it!—Oh, I suppose I was sold a bill of goods about the Resurrection, but aside from that, never happier!"

So much for Eternity, I thought, and took a sip; if I understood him correctly—and it turned out that I had—he was saying that such things as the Resurrection of Christ, or the reality of life after death, ought not to be taken too literally. "I know of no reputable theologian," he said, "who is willing to support the idea of a physical resurrection."

Old Father John heard what he said. The argument which followed was mainly Father John shouting, "Confect the Eucharist!" and "Resurrection!" and Pete Peterson shouting, "Bill of goods! Bill of goods!" In the end Father Pete decided to leave before "somebody clubbed somebody" and pushed himself out past Tommy Fiacre, who was back at the doorway, and headed for bed early. But as he left he shouted, "I am leaving you guys to your ignorance. *Let the dead bury their dead!*"

The evening was a shambles; our houseguest gone, everyone with any sense retired; that left only Father John with myself and Brother Timothy. And I realized that I should not be there at all; at last I realized that I *had* left, in every way but physically. At some moment in the preceding weeks I had gone, had done it; perhaps when I had signed my name to the apartment lease, or maybe it was when I had touched the brakes in the small town of Pembroke, to go up the courthouse steps and ask, with many clearings of the throat, how a person went about getting married. Or was it much earlier, in some seminar on James Joyce or on the poems of William Butler Yeats when I looked out over student heads and knew that I no longer believed?

But Father John was deeply moved, over and above the drink. I could see him rise slowly on shaky legs and steady himself, so that I held out my two hands to catch him lest he fall. And in the same voice in which he had uttered it in so many great churches across the country, he pronounced the words,

> "If the Son of Man be not risen from the Dead
> —If He be not truly risen—
> Then is our Faith in vain
> And we, among all men,
> Are the most miserable!"

I think I must have turned away, to see, perhaps, if my drink was safe. But I took my eyes off him for a moment, and while I did so, he slipped sideways, bumping the doorpost hard, then sliding quickly to the floor.

We jumped up, Timothy and I, to get him to his room, Timothy at the feet and me at the head (we had done it before). But on the stairs he came to in a new mood, singing *"Par—ops—si—day—in—Par—ooops—ee—day"* until we laid him safely down. I kissed him on the forehead, and wondered if he knew I was leaving. At any rate, Father John would rise in the morning without a hangover, forgetting everything that had happened. He always did.

When we returned, I had my car keys in my hand, but Father De Angelis, the Assistant Superior, wanted to know what was going on. "What's this?" he asked, pointing to a red smudge on the doorjamb.

"Father John passed out," I said. "We put him to bed; he'll be all right."

Father De Angelis looked at me. I knew what he was thinking. Suddenly a feeling of terror came over me— some of it was the drink, of course, and yet it was more than that, for it was as much terror as I have ever known. I was afraid that he was going to order me off to bed; but it was not just that he was going to order me back to my old cell, it was not that. It was that I felt within myself that if he did so, I might still obey.

Instead, Father De Angelis tried to remove the mark from the door frame, shook his head, and glided off.

I responded like a crazy man. I grabbed some pita bread off the sideboard and stuffed it into my mouth; I felt for my car keys and ran for my old car, though I was in no shape to drive. As I ran, I felt something funny: I had sandals on, and wondered if I could drive with them on my feet.

"North," I said, slowly reading the signs at the entrance to the Expressway. "The Drinking Gourd," I said to myself. "Jes' follow the Drinking Gourd!" I knew I had to go north, then east on Route 128, then south on #3 to get to Hingham, where my apartment was, and safety. But I got lost; I was in Cohasset; I remember Egypt Road, and Jerusalem Road, and the surf pounding up over the rocks. Then I was in Hingham, around Hingham Harbor and the rotary. That was when the police lights lit up from behind.

"Have you been drinking?" a young police officer asked, in through the window. There was another officer behind him, and they both carried enormous flashlights. The Civil Arm.

Who, me? Only for liturgical purposes. Purely sacramental. "No," I said in an honest tone.

"You have been driving over the line. You made a U-turn back there in front of the police cruiser! Let me see your license." The powerful beam of the flashlight was focused upon the little plastic card with my face on it, my name and Social Security number, everything, even the initials of the Order, "I.H.S.," and of course the Roman collar.

There was a pause. He consulted with the second officer. He returned, the other officer looking over his shoulder. "Are you a priest?" he asked. The tone was conciliatory, but the flashlight was dancing all over the night sky, and when it hit my eyes directly, the beam seemed to come through and touch the back of my skull and interrogate me over and over with the same question.

"No," I said. "I was. —I used to be."

There was another pause, and the flashlight went out. In the dark, one of the officers said, "Where do you live? Where is your place of residence?"

"Queen Anne's Gate apartments—just up there." I pointed where I thought they were.

Relief on the part of the Civil Arm: another jurisdiction entirely, just over the line. A new "cahoots" tone: "Look, there's a coffee shop on the next corner. Just stop and get a cup of coffee, then go on home to your apartment, you'll be all right."

I took a sandal off the brake and placed it very deliberately on the gas; I eased forward slowly, the police cruiser following at a respectful distance; they followed me for only half a block, I saw their lights swerve with great decisiveness off onto another street. I never did find the coffee shop, but I got home, to my new home, safely.

That ended the foolishness; from then on everything was out in the open. I took our college president to an Italian restaurant and explained what I was going to do; he was decent—I remember him saying, "There will be mornings when you will wonder if it is all worth it": he taught Economics, and knew better than I did the hard realities of the situation.

In the apartment I waited one day for the electric meter to be turned on, and another for the telephone to be installed. I lived on ham sandwiches, rye bread, and a jar of pickles. In the afternoon I slipped out and made my first purchase, which I thought was at a good price and sensible—six water glasses. I am afraid they are the kind that years ago used to be given away free by gasoline stations to get you to buy more gasoline, and they have been rejected by every person of taste who has passed through our kitchen. There are only four of them left, and Anne Francis has pushed them way back on the top shelf. When I see them I try to remember what I was like the afternoon I went out to buy them. And when I see them I know that I would not have the courage or the energy ever again to do what I did that time.

With the power on and while I was waiting for the phone man, I installed my hi-fi system, a thing of wires and bareness, so that there would be music in the new place, carefully scraping the copper wires, and attaching positives and negatives. I flipped the switch; one of Boston's interminable Irish programs was on: the Clancy Brothers and Tommy Makem were singing "Wild

Mountain Thyme," the rich, soft voice of Tommy Makem singing out the words, "Will ye go, Lassie, go?" "And we'll all go together," he kept singing,

> "And we'll all go together—
> To pull Wild Mountain Thyme
> All around the blooming heather—
> Will ye go, Lassie, go?"

Someone asked Anne Francis once where she first met me. "We grew up together," she said, and it is still the best answer. Hers is a harsher story than mine, which I must let her tell elsewhere: elected Superior again and again by her order of nuns, fighting to frame a constitution to allow them growth and maturity until she could fight Rome no more. We left separately, each for private reasons. She was filled with life; the Germans have a saying: "You could *steal horses* with a girl like that!"

If someone asked me where I met Anne Francis, I would say, "At airports: London, Dublin, O'Hare, Logan." She came to me out of the clouds, out of the blue, out of the fog. I would wait at numbered gates, which speck was she? Closely watched specks. One speck on the ground. God in the clouds: will these two specks get together? I thought of flaming wreckage, ice on the wings, cloud canyons. Then I would get the right speck: in over the fence, flare-out, burst of blue smoke as the rubber burned on the runway. I even watched the landing gear to see if it held.

We talked over dinner at airport restaurants, wine as we could afford, detailed how things were going.

Then to another gate, another airline. Goodbye. I to a vantage point, where I watched her become a speck again.

And I would go home to countless cold rooms where the spirit had gone out. Tiny, tiny speck; how could so much be held in so small?

One day when we met she said, "I have written to Rome. I said, 'Thank you for bringing me to the truth of my own reality. I will no longer pay homage to that in which I do not believe.' " She went back one last time to conclude things; we had both pretty much made up our minds.

Finally, late in the afternoon, the phone man came to my apartment; he took an intolerable time installing the phone line. He talked about fishing for striped bass. He went over everything twice, and pronounced it usable. I signed his work pad, showed him out. When he was gone, I rushed to the telephone, dialed the well-memorized number, and when Anne Francis answered, I said,

"Will ye go, Lassie, go?"

Francis Phelan, who was born in Pittsburgh and educated at Notre Dame and University College Dublin, lives with his wife Anne Francis Cavanaugh in a restored house near the Bunker Hill monument in old Charlestown, where he has built a roof-top deck and city garden. His fiction has appeared in the *Georgia Review*, the *Southern Review*, and *The New Yorker*; and he was awarded a Pushcart Prize in 1982. He teaches literature and writing at Stonehill College, and is working on a second novel.

Printed in the United States
1087200002B/121-138

9 780743 245371